THE YEARS, MONTHS, DAYS

YAN LIANKE

THE YEARS, MONTHS, DAYS

Two Novellas

Translated from the Chinese by
Carlos Rojas

Black Cat
New York

The Years, Months, Days first published in China in 1997
as *Nian yue ri* by *Harvest* magazine

Marrow first published in China in 2001 as *Balou tiange*
by Beiyue Literature & Art Publishing House, Beijing
Translation from the original Chinese by Carlos Rojas first published in English in 2015 by Penguin Group (Australia) in association with Penguin (Beijing) Ltd.
Copyright © 2001 by Yan Lianke
Translation copyright © 2015 by Penguin Group (Australia) in association with Penguin (Beijing) Ltd.

Published simultaneously in Canada
Printed in the United States of America

First Grove Atlantic paperback edition: December 2017

Library of Congress Cataloging-in-Publication data available for this title.

ISBN 978-0-8021-2665-8
eISBN 978-0-8021-8881-6

Black Cat
an imprint of Grove Atlantic
154 West 14th Street
New York, NY 10011

Distributed by Publishers Group West

groveatlantic.com

17 18 19 20   10 9 8 7 6 5 4 3 2 1

Contents

Translator's Note

"When I was young," Yan Lianke writes in a recent essay, "hunger constantly followed me around, like a tail."*

Yan Lianke is known for his unconventional use of analogy. In his work, colors and smells, emotions and motivations, and even sunrays and moonlight are often treated as though they have a material existence. In this particular description of his youth, he compares his hunger to a corporeal appendage—albeit a body part that humans don't actually have in the first place. In likening his hunger to a tail, Yan emphasizes not only its immediacy but also its phantasmic character—a yearning so acute that it is perceived as though it were a concrete presence in its own right.

* Yan Lianke, "*Kongju yu beipan jiang yu wo zhongsheng tongxing*" (Terror and betrayal will follow me throughout my life), in *Chenmo yu chuanxi* (Silence and breath) (Taipei: Ink Literary Monthly, 2014), 127–150: 129.

For the young Yan Lianke, hunger was indeed a fact of life. The author was born in rural Henan province in 1958, which happened to be the first year of the national campaign known as the Great Leap Forward. Initially conceived as China's second Five-Year Plan, the Great Leap Forward sought to jump-start the nation's economic development, permitting it to quickly overtake developed nations like Britain. In reality, the campaign's policies resulted in a devastating famine that claimed the lives of tens of millions of Chinese. Known officially (and euphemistically) as the Three Years of Natural Disaster, the Great Famine that consumed China during Yan's childhood had far-reaching implications for both the nation and the people who lived through it. Although Yan's novel *The Four Books* is his only work that is explicitly set during the period of the Great Famine, many of his other works reflect on related themes of hunger and loss, yearning and desire.

The Years, Months, Days unfolds during an acute drought afflicting a remote community in the author's home province of Henan, in central China. The drought results in a mass exodus, and the only resident who stays behind is a seventy-two-year-old man identified simply as the Elder, who fears he wouldn't survive the journey. The Elder devotes himself to raising a corn seedling he planted, so that the other villagers might have food when they eventually return. His only companion throughout this time is a blind dog, and the Elder's remarks to the dog and his comments to himself frequently bleed into one another as they both struggle desperately to survive. In this way, the Elder comes to view the dog as both an extension of himself, but also as an external projection of his own hunger.

Marrow also revolves around the specter of hunger. The novella focuses on a family with four children. The three sisters each suffer from epilepsy and other ailments, and when their younger brother is a year and a half old he, too, begins displaying similar symptoms. The boy's parents take him to see a doctor, who concludes that all four children have inherited their condition from their father (who happens to be asymptomatic). Despondent upon realizing that he is the source of his children's illness, the father commits suicide, leaving his wife to raise the children on her own. Although the story unfolds two decades after the father's death, his widow continues to interact with her husband as though he were still alive—particularly with respect to issues of how to raise their children. By this point, the mother has already succeeded in marrying off her two eldest daughters, but is still struggling to find a suitable husband for her third daughter, while also attempting to domesticate her son's deviant desires—which include incestuous and even zoophilic impulses. In the end, the novella explores the boy's more literal hunger and its possible reconfiguration.

Underlying the themes of food and hunger in these two works are related concerns with identity and alterity. In *The Years, Months, Days*, the Elder develops a peculiar symbiotic relationship with the blind dog, whom he comes to view as a virtual extension of himself even as it becomes increasingly clear that there is insufficient food to feed both of them. A parallel, and inverse, figure can be found in the wolves that the Elder encounters near a small pool that is one of his only remaining sources of fresh water. The Elder and the wolves are united by their shared hunger, even as that same hunger leaves them in a deadly stalemate that threatens the Elder's very existence.

Yan Lianke recounts a similar face-off at the beginning of the essay in which he compares his childhood hunger to a tail. Yan opens with a description of how, one day when he was four or five, he encountered a wolf in the doorway of his home. The animal appeared emaciated, and Yan initially assumed it was merely a hungry dog. His first impulse, accordingly, was to try to feed it, despite the fact that he didn't even have food for himself. Yan and the wolf simply stood there staring at each other, and it was not until the other villagers returned and drove the animal away that Yan finally realized that his unexpected visitor was, in fact, a wolf. Yan subsequently came to view the wolf with a combination of fear and love—recognizing that the predator could easily have attacked him, but also feeling deeply moved by the animal's gentle expression. In this description of the famished wolf, and in the hunger-as-tail analogy that immediately follows it, the wolf and the tail both function as a sort of phantom limb—an external manifestation of the author's hunger and a vicarious projection of the author himself.

In their focus on solitude and loneliness, the two novellas included in this volume are shaped by similar phantasmic logic, in that they both explore the transformation of absence into spectral presence. In both works the natural world becomes endowed with a set of distinctly anthropomorphic qualities, and conditions of extreme deprivation encourage a radical reassessment of the protagonists' understanding of themselves and the world they inhabit.

—Carlos Rojas

THE YEARS, MONTHS, DAYS

In the year of the great drought, time was baked to ash; and if you tried to grab the sun, it would stick to your palm like charcoal. One sun after another passed overhead, and from dawn till dusk, the Elder could hear his own hair burning. Occasionally he would reach up to the sky, and could smell the stench of burned fingernails. *Damn this sky!* He always cursed this way as he emerged from the empty village and stepped into the interminable loneliness. He peered side-eyed at the sun, then announced, *Blindy, let's go.* His blind dog followed his faint footsteps, and like a pair of shadows they left the village.

The Elder climbed the mountain, stomping the sunlight under his feet. The rays of light shining down from the eastern ridge pounded his face, his hands, and his feet like bamboo canes. His face was burning as though it had been slapped, and as the corners of his eyes met the deep wrinkles on his cheeks, the fiery red pain seemed to conceal countless pearls like glowing embers.

The Elder went to take a piss.

The blind dog followed him.

For half a month, the first thing the Elder and the dog would do every morning after they woke up was to go to Baliban Hill, to take a piss. On the side of the hill facing the sun, there was a corn seedling the Elder had planted. There was only this single seedling, standing alone in the middle of this devastating drought—and under the searing sun it appeared so green that it was as though the color were dripping off it. When the seedling lacked water, it relied on the Elder's and the dog's urine that had accumulated overnight. The Elder saw that the seedling appeared to have grown another three fingers taller since the day before, and where it had previously only had four leaves, now it had five. His heart started pounding and he felt a surge of warmth in his chest, as a smile rippled across his face. The seedling grew only one leaf at a time, and the Elder wondered why scholar trees, elm trees, and toon trees all grew two leaves at a time?

The Elder turned to his blind dog and asked, *Why is it that the leaves of trees and crops grow differently?* He gazed at the dog's head and then, without waiting for the dog to answer, he turned and left, continuing to reflect as he walked away. The Elder looked up, held his hand to his forehead, and traced the sun's rays. In the distance, he saw the bare mountain ridge glistening purple, as though there were a thick layer of smoke on the ground. The Elder knew this was nighttime air being released from the soil by the heat of the sun.

The villagers had all resolved to flee. As a result of the drought, the wheat in the fields had died, the mountain peaks had been left barren, and the entire world had withered. The daily hopes of the villagers had also dried up. The drought had continued until the autumn sowing season, when suddenly there was a downpour and the streets were filled with the sound of pounding drums. Everyone had been shouting, "Autumn sowing . . . autumn sowing! Heaven has given us an autumn sowing season!" Adults shouted, children shouted, men shouted, and women shouted as though they were performing in an opera—their delighted voices flowed down the streets of the village, from east to west, from west to east, and then from the village over to the mountain ridge.

"It's autumn sowing season."

"It's autumn sowing season."

"Heaven has given us rain, to let us proceed with the autumn sowing."

These shouts, by both young and old, shook the entire mountain range. Sparrows that had alighted on tree branches were startled from their perches and flew away, their feathers drifting down like snow. Chickens and pigs stood astonished in the doorways of houses, their faces pale with shock. The oxen in cattle sheds suddenly started tugging at the ropes tied to their snouts, as their nostrils were ripped open and dark blood flowed into the feed troughs. All the cats and dogs crawled up onto the roofs of houses and gazed down at the villagers in terror.

For three days in a row, clouds grew increasingly dense.

Everyone from Liujiajian Village, Wujiahe Village, Qianliang Village, Houliang Village, Shuanmazhuang Village—in short, everyone from the entire Balou Mountain region—took the corn seed they had stored and rushed to sow their fields.

Three days later, the clouds dispersed, and the searing sun once again bore down on the mountain ridge like a fire.

Six months later, half of the villagers locked their doors and courtyard gates, and fled the drought. Over the next three days and two nights, a steady stream of refugees fled. The crowd of refugees grew like ants relocating to another anthill, as they surged along the road behind the village, heading out into the world. The sound of their footsteps echoed back to the village, pounding on the doors and windows of every house.

The Elder had been one of the last to decide to leave. That was the ninth day of the sixth lunar month, and the Elder gathered with a group of several dozen other villagers. The villagers asked, "Where should we go?" The Elder replied, "Let's go east." The villagers said, "What is in the east?" The Elder replied that east was the direction of Xuzhou, and in three to ten days they could make it there and live comfortably. They all headed east. The burning sun pounded the mountain road and plumes of dust rose every time they took a step. When they reached Baliban Field, however, the Elder stopped. He went and peed behind his field, then returned and told the other villagers, "You should go on. Continue heading east."

"What about you?"

"A corn plant has sprouted in my field."

"Will a single corn plant keep you from starving, Elder?"

"I'm seventy-two years old, and would surely die of exhaustion if I tried to walk for three days. If I'm going to die either way, I'd prefer to die in my own village."

The other villagers left. They drifted away like a dark mass, and under the searing sun they disappeared into a cloud of dust. The Elder stood at the end of his field until they vanished from sight, at which point a feeling of solitude struck his heart with a thud. His entire body began to tremble, as he suddenly realized that he, a seventy-two-year-old man, was now the only living soul in the entire village—and perhaps even the entire mountain range. There was a vast emptiness in his heart, as a sense of stillness and desolation enveloped his body.

On that morning, as the sun was changing from yellow to red as it passed over the eastern mountains, the Elder and his dog had gone out to Baliban Field as usual. From a distance, the Elder saw that in the center of this field, the corn seedling—which was already as tall as a chopstick—appeared as green as a drop of water under the red sun. He turned and asked the blind dog, *Can you smell it?* Then added, *It's so fragrant, you can smell it from countless* li *away.* The blind dog angled its head up to him, rubbed his leg, then silently ran over to the seedling.

Ahead of them was a deep gully, from which trapped heat surged out and singed the Elder's cheeks. The Elder removed his white shirt, rolled it into a ball, and wiped his face. He could smell the reek of sweat three to five inches deep. *This would make excellent fertilizer,* he thought. *I'll let this seedling grow for another month, then I'll wash my shirt, bring the waste water to the field, and let the seedling enjoy it as though it were a*

New Year's feast. The Elder held his shirt under his armpits, like a precious treasure. The seedling appeared before him. It was one palm tall, had five leaves, but had not yet produced the bud the Elder was hoping for. He examined the top of the seedling, brushing away some dust as a feeling of disappointment welled up in his heart.

The dog rubbed against the Elder's leg. It walked once around the seedling, then again. The Elder said, *Blindy, go away.* The dog stopped and barked several times like a dried tangerine peel, then lifted its head toward the Elder, as though there were something it urgently had to do.

The Elder knew that the dog needed to pee. He went over to an old scholar tree and fetched his hoe—the Elder always hung his tools there when he wasn't using them—then went back and dug a small hole on the west side of the seedling—the previous day it had been the east side. He told the dog, *OK, go ahead and pee.*

Before the Elder could check to see if the dog had finished urinating, the seventy-two-year-old man's eyes were struck by something. His eyes hurt, his heart began to pound, when he saw that the seedling's lowest two leaves had developed some tiny black dots, as though they were covered in tiny wheat grain shells. *Are these dry spots? Each morning I come to pee and each evening I bring the seedling water. How could it be suffering from dryness?* Just as he was standing up again, the dog's yellow urine struck his head. It occurred to him that those dots were not a result of dryness, but rather were an indication that the fertilizer was too strong. Dog urine is much fattier than human urine, and also much warmer. The Elder complained, *Blindy,*

I'll fuck your ancestors, yet you still insist on peeing. He lashed out with his foot and violently kicked the dog, which landed several feet away like a sack of millet. *I told you to pee,* the Elder shouted, *but you deliberately tried to burn the seedling, didn't you?*

The dog stood there, its well-like eye sockets staring blankly.

The Elder said, *Serves you right.* With an angry glance, he squatted down, held the tender leaves, and carefully inspected the black dots on their jade-like surface. He quickly reached over and grabbed some white foam from the dog's urine, which had not yet been fully absorbed by the soil, and tossed it away. Next he used his hoe to refill the hole with several handfuls of the urine-mud, then said to the dog, *Let's go. Let's go fetch some water. If we don't get water to dilute this fertilizer, in less than two days the seedling will have burned up.*

The dog continued along the original path toward the mountain ridge, and the Elder followed it—his footsteps sounding like withered leaves landing under the hot sun. However, the seedling's crisis resembled the Elder's and the dog's footsteps—it followed them away, then followed them back.

After the seedling's sixth leaf appeared, the Elder went to fetch some water, but as he was on his way to the well a sudden breeze blew off his straw hat. The hat rolled down the street, and the Elder ran after it.

That breeze started off slow, then gradually picked up speed, forming a little twister. As a result, the hat always remained a foot ahead of the Elder, who chased it all the way to the village entrance. Several times he just barely managed to touch the hat, but the twister always pulled it away again.

The Elder was seventy-two years old, and his legs were not as strong as before. He thought to himself, *I don't even want this hat anymore. How about that? I'm the only person left in this entire village. I could easily go into anyone's house and find myself another one.* The Elder looked up, and saw a solitary house on the mountain ridge—like a temple on the side of the road. The twister bumped against that wall, and stopped moving.

The Elder walked slowly to the wall and kicked at the twister a few times. Then he leaned over, picked up the hat, and tore it apart. He threw the pieces to the ground and stomped on them while shouting,

I told you to run away!

I told you to go with the twister.

I don't want to have to keep waiting for you to leave.

After the Elder tore the hat to pieces, the fresh scent of the straw slowly dissipated. Along that mountain ridge, which had endured scorching weather for so many days, there now appeared a new scent. The Elder rolled what remained of the hat into a ball, then threw it down and stomped on it again, exclaiming, *Aren't you going to run away? This way, you'll never be able to run away. The sun and the drought want to torture me, and even your fucking mother wants to torture me.* As he was saying this, the Elder took a deep breath, then gazed at the hillside beyond Baliban Field. As he was looking, his feet stopped stomping on the remainder of the straw hat, and his mumblings were also cut short like a rope.

Over by the hill, the mountains and plain were covered with fiery red dust, like a translucent wall that swayed back and forth. The Elder stared in disbelief, realizing that what he had seen was actually not a little twister but rather a major wind. As he stood in front of the wall under the searing sun, his heart pounded, as though the wall had collapsed and was crushing him.

He started to rush over to Baliban Hill.

In the distance, the wall of translucent dust began to thicken. It rose and swayed, as though it were the beginning of a flood that was about to bury the entire mountain range.

The Elder reflected, *It's over!* He was afraid this was really the end. *When that twister blew my hat off, it was actually leading me over to the mountain! It wanted to tell me that a strong wind had developed on the hill.* He continued, *I'm afraid I let you down, little twister. I really shouldn't have kicked you.* He continued, *There's also my straw hat. It had no qualms about going wherever the little twister was blowing it, so why did I have to rip it up? I'm getting old—really old. I may even be getting a bit senile, and am having trouble distinguishing right from wrong.* These self-recriminations sprouted from his mouth like a continuous vine. As he began to calm down, the wind started to subside, as did the pounding in his ears—although the sudden silence left him with a piercing pain in his eardrums. The sunlight also regained its earlier dynamism, becoming strong and hard. The rays generated a clear, white squeaking sound in the fields, as though bean pods were exploding under the searing heat of the sun. The Elder's pace slowed, and his panting subsided. When he reached the hill, he stood at the front of his field, and his breath was cut off by the scene before him.

The seedling had nearly been blown over by the wind, and was now trembling like a broken finger. Under the hard sunlight, a dense green sorrow was flowing like a silk thread.

The Elder and the dog decided to relocate to Baliban Hill.

The Elder didn't hesitate and, like an old melon farmer who has to live in his melon field when the melons are about to ripen, he relocated to the field. He planted four posts in the ground next to the seedling, placed a couple of wooden doors on top of the posts, and draped four straw mats over them, making a simple shed. Then he hammered some nails to the posts, from which he hung his pot, spoon, and brush. He stuffed his bowls into a flour bag, and hung it under the pot. Finally, he dug a hole for a small oven in the ground under the cliff. Then, he simply waited for the seedling to sprout more leaves.

Given that the Elder had moved to a new location, when night fell he simply couldn't fall asleep. The moonlike white heat was moving through the air. He removed his underwear, which was all that he had been wearing, and sat naked on the bed, smoking. Under the dim light of the pipe, he found himself gazing at that thing between his legs, which was dangling there like a lantern. Finding it extremely ugly, he put his underwear back on and thought, *I am truly old—that is no longer of any use to me, and is no longer capable of bringing me pleasure. It isn't even as valuable to me as the corn seedling. Every single leaf of the seedling gives me enjoyment, like the women standing in the field or chatting next to the well, whom I would admire when I was young.* A languid feeling coursed through his body and he emptied the bowl of his pipe, as the embers fell onto the dark field. Then he woke up the blind dog sleeping next to him.

The Elder asked, *Are you awake?*

Then he added, *You're blind, yet you are sleeping so soundly. Meanwhile, I can see, yet I can't fall asleep.*

The dog crawled over to lick the Elder's hand, and the Elder caressed its head, running his fingers through its fur. As he was smoothing the dog's fur, he noticed that a pair of bright tears had appeared in the animal's empty eye sockets. The Elder wiped away the tears, and said, *This sun, which refuses to die, truly has a black heart. It even burned this dog's eyes.* Upon remembering how the dog's eyes had been seared by the sun, the Elder felt something tugging at his heart. He pulled the dog over and caressed its eyes, as the animal's tears drenched his hand like a pair of mountain springs. *This is something no one could possibly have expected,* the Elder thought. Every time there was a drought, people would always erect an altar at the front of the village and would leave three plates of offerings and two jugs. The jugs would always be full of water, and would have two dragons painted on the side. Then, the villagers would leave a dog tied between the two jugs, and have the dog look up at the sky. When the dog was thirsty they would give it water, and when it was hungry they would give it food, but when it was neither hungry or thirsty they would simply let it bark furiously at the sun. In the past, they would have let this continue for at least three and at most seven days, until the sun eventually retreated in the face of the dog's barks, and there would be wind, rain, or cloudy skies. But this year, they brought in a wild dog from outside the village and tied it in front of the altar, and although the dog barked for half a month, the sun continued to burn bright, rising and setting every day on schedule. Finally, at noon on the sixteenth day, the Elder walked past the altar and noticed that one of the jugs was bone-dry and the bottom of the other was smoldering. The Elder looked at the dog, and saw that its fur was matted together, and when it opened its mouth no sound came out.

The Elder released the dog, and said, *You can leave. It's not going to rain.*

The dog came down from the altar. It took a few steps, then ran into a wall. It turned around, then ran into a tree. The Elder went and grabbed the dog's ear to take a look, and his heart skipped a beat as he realized the dog's eyes had gotten scorched by the sun, and all that was left was a pair of sockets as empty as dry wells.

The Elder had decided to keep the dog.

Now, the Elder thought, *It's fortunate I decided to keep this blind dog, because otherwise I would have been left alone here in the mountains, and who would I have had to talk to?* The weather was getting cooler, as the daytime heat began to subside. The moon and stars overhead began to regain their brightness. There was a sound like water flowing, but the Elder knew that this sound was not from water, nor was it from the trees, the grass, or from insects, but rather from the empty sky itself, which produced a sound of silence out of its extreme stillness. He continued caressing the dog's head, then dragged his hand down its back and patted its rear. Then he returned his hand to the dog's head, by which point the dog was no longer crying. The Elder caressed the animal's fur with one hand, as the dog licked his other hand. That night, the two of them were enveloped by a warm sense of shared fate.

The Elder said, *Blindy, we should live together. Don't you agree? Life is more interesting with a companion.*

The dog licked his palm.

The Elder said, *I don't have much longer to live. If you could keep me company until I die, then I'd be able to die a good death.*

The dog moved from licking the man's fingers to licking his wrist, which seemed to be interminably long.

He said, *Blindy, do you think our corn seedling will bud again?* The dog stopped licking his hand, then nodded. He asked, *Will it bud tonight, or tomorrow? I'm sleepy. Don't nod, because I can't see you anyway. Just answer me—do you think it will bud tomorrow, or tonight?* The Elder leaned against the shed wall and closed his eyes, and the darkness covered his face like a piece of wet gauze. He stopped caressing the dog's back, and his hand came to rest on the dog's head as he fell asleep.

When the Elder woke up, the sun was already three rod-lengths in the sky. He felt a searing pain under his eyelids, so he sat up and rubbed his eyes. When he gazed out at the golden orb that was still hanging there, he cursed, *Fuck your ancestors for eight generations. Watch how one day I'm not going to dig your family's grave.* After this, he noticed that the blind dog was lying next to the corn seedling in the middle of the field. He had a sudden suspicion, and asked, *Has it budded?* The dog nodded, then the Elder climbed out of the shed. When he reached the seedling, he saw that it did indeed have a new bud. The seedling resembled a newly sprouted cassia tree—it was half a finger tall, so tender it seemed as though it would topple over at the slightest touch, and in the sunlight it appeared as glossy as jade.

The Elder wanted to place something over the sprout to shield it from the sun, so he went down to the gully and looked around, but couldn't find anything and eventually returned empty-handed. He stood next to the stove for a while, then grabbed the hoe and walked over to the pagoda tree and broke off a branch, which he brought back and carefully placed over the sprout. Next he climbed onto the shed, retrieved his shirt, and draped it over the branch, so that the sprout could have some shade.

He said, *I can't bear to have another accident.*

He added, *Blindy, you should eat something. What would you like?*

Then he said, *What is there to eat in the morning? Shall we have some corn soup? Then we can cook something tasty for lunch.*

After the sprout grew two new leaves, the Elder returned to the village to look for something to eat. There wasn't a single grain of wheat in his home. He thought that in such a large village, even if each household had only a handful of grain or a pinch of flour, this would be enough for him and the blind dog to survive this devastating drought. However, when he returned to the village, he discovered that the door to each house was locked, and there were cobwebs everywhere. He returned to his own house. He knew perfectly well that the flour jug had already been swept clean, but he still peered inside, then reached in and felt around. After he pulled out his hand, he stuck his fingers in his mouth and sucked on them, and the pure white taste of wheat blossomed in his mouth and surged through his body. He took a deep breath and inhaled the fragrant scent, then went outside and stood in the street. The sun's rays shone down, flowing through the village like a river of gold. In the deathly silence, the Elder heard the sound of sunlight dripping from the roof. He thought indignantly, *Everyone in the entire mountain ridge has fled, and the thieves have either starved to death or died of thirst. Did all of you fucking lock your doors just to stymie me? I'll climb your walls and pry open your doors, and find who has left behind any grain. If you didn't store any grain, then what had you been planning to eat during the drought? And if you didn't leave behind any grain, then why the hell did you bother to lock your doors in the first place?* The Elder stood in the doorway of one family's house. This house belonged to one of his nephews, with whom he shared a surname. The Elder headed to another house, and stopped in the doorway of an old widow's residence. When the widow was younger, she would give the Elder a pair of thick-soled boots every winter. Now she was dead, and her son had inherited this compound. The thought of this house gave the Elder a warm feeling that lingered in his empty heart. The Elder studied the door for a while, then continued on. His footsteps were lonely but resonant, like wood being chopped in the forest. The sound echoed past each family's locked door, flowing by his feet like a dried-up boat. The Elder finally made it through the entire village, by which point the sun had reached its zenith. It was time for lunch, and he mumbled to himself, *If only Blindy were here, then whichever house it told me to break into, I'd immediately scale the wall and go inside.*

The Elder faced the mountain ridge and shouted, *Blindy . . . Blindy! Whose house do you think I should break into?*

The only response the Elder received was deafening silence. Discouraged, the Elder sat down and smoked his pipe. Then, he returned empty-handed to Baliban Hill. When the Elder approached, the blind dog wagged its tail, then ran up, following his voice, and rubbed its head on his pants. The Elder ignored the dog, and instead went over to the pagoda tree to fetch his hoe. He went to the shed to get a bowl and proceeded to dig a hole. After digging two or three more holes, the Elder finally unearthed a seed he had previously planted. It was golden yellow and completely intact, and was heated by the sun's rays to the point that it burned his hand. The Elder then dug a series of holes at the same intervals at which he had originally planted the seeds, and from each hole he unearthed one or two seeds. By the time he had traversed half the ridge, his bowl was full of seeds.

In this way, he was able to enjoy a dish of fried corn seeds.

As he was eating his fried seeds, the Elder sat with the blind dog under the shadow of the shed and began to chuckle. *Every family has stored some food for me,* he remarked, *so if I go out into the field and dig for a day, I could find enough for the two of us to eat for three more days.* When he did go to another family's fields, however, he found the situation wasn't so simple. He didn't know where exactly the other family had planted their seeds, and didn't know where exactly he should dig. Many families, as they rushed to sow their corn before the rains came, had their children grab hoes and start digging frantically, and the result was that the seeds were planted at different depths and at irregular intervals—not at all like the Elder's perfectly even and regularly spaced holes. In the past, families would never have permitted their children to hoe, but during this drought everything had gotten confused.

As a result, the Elder found that he couldn't dig for one day and obtain sufficient food for him and the dog to survive on for another three days. Instead, he would exert himself all day, and if he was fortunate he'd find enough grain for two days, and if not he'd only end up with enough for one day. His sprout continued to grow, and in the still night it produced a faint and tender sound, like the quiet breathing of a sleeping baby. The Elder and the dog were sitting next to the sprout, resting after having spent all day digging. When they heard the sprout breathing, their joints suddenly felt warm and relaxed. The moon emerged, as round as a woman's face, and hung overhead. The stars sparkled all around it, like buttons on new clothing worn for New Year's, fastened to an unimaginably vast blue silk cloth. At that moment, the Elder suddenly asked the dog, *Blindy, when you were younger, did you do it with a lot of female dogs?*

The dog stared at him blankly.

If you don't want to answer, so be it. The Elder sighed, then lit his pipe. He said to the sky, *It's good to be young. When you're young, you have energy, and at night you can have a woman. If she is very bright, then when you return from the fields, she'll bring you some water; if your face is covered in sweat, she'll hand you a fan; and when it snows, she'll warm up your bedding for you. If you don't sleep soundly with her at night, then when you wake up in the morning she'll urge you to go back to sleep.* The Elder took a long drag on his pipe, then exhaled a cloud of smoke like a long embankment. While patting the dog, he asked, *How is that sort of life any different from that of gods and deities?*

The Elder continued, *Have you lived that sort of life, Blindy?* The dog was silent.

The Elder said, *Tell me, Blindy, was it not for that sort of life that men came into this world?* The Elder didn't wait for the dog to respond, and instead answered his own question, *I would say yes.* Then he added, *But not when we're old. When we're old, we only live for a tree, a tuft of grass, or a passel of grandchildren. Living, after all, is better than dying.* As the Elder said this, he took another drag on his pipe, and in the dim light he noticed that the sound the corn sprout was making as it grew was reaching out toward his ear like a tender thread. He leaned toward the sprout, and saw that the top, which was already more than knee-high, appeared disheveled. A new leaf was budding from the pale purplish-yellow stem. There were already nine leaves arching out from the corn sprout like bent bows. The Elder stood up, grabbed his hoe, and dug a hole below the sprout. He and the blind dog both urinated into the hole, filling it with three bowls of urine, then refilled it with dirt. Next, he mixed some dirt and water, and made a small pile of mud around the corn sprout. He was afraid that another gust of wind might blow the sprout over, so that night the Elder returned to the village to fetch four reed mats, then erected four poles around the sprout at intervals of four feet, and placed the mats against the poles to form an enclosure. As he was positioning the mats, the Elder said, *Blindy, go to the village and find some rope or string. Any kind will do.* The blind dog zigzagged down the mountain path, and finally, as the moon was setting and the stars were beginning to fade, it returned, holding in its mouth the remains of the Elder's ripped-up straw hat. The Elder used the hat's string to fasten the mats to the poles, and when he ran out of string he used the black thread from his own pants. By the time he had finished, the eastern sky was beginning to brighten.

Between dawn and dusk, that ring of mats surrounded the corn sprout like a small garden in front of the house of a wealthy peasant. The solitary sprout stood there like a flagpole. It was able to enjoy a privileged existence, drinking water and absorbing nutrients, and at midday it was shaded by the reed mats. The sprout grew crazily, and after a week or so it had already reached the top of the enclosure.

The problem was that the sun kept reappearing, and the well would inevitably dry up. The Elder returned to the village every day to fetch some water, and each trip he would have to lower the bucket into the well more than ten times, but even then would end up with half a bucket of sand and murky water. A feeling of terror began to rise out of the well, permeating the Elder's entire being. Finally, one day he lowered the bucket, using the entire length of the rope, but only managed to bring up the equivalent of a small bowl of water. He then had to wait for a long time before another bowlful of water seeped into the bottom of the well.

The well was almost dry, like a tree that had lost all its leaves.

The Elder came up with an idea—before nightfall he lowered his quilt into the well, let it sit there overnight, then the next morning he hauled it up and was able to wring out half a bucketful of water. He then lowered the quilt back into the well, and took the water to the field. He also took the water from washing dishes, from washing his face, and from occasionally washing his clothes—and used it to irrigate the corn sprout. In this way, he managed to make do, and his water supply did not appear excessively limited. As he was again wringing the water from the quilt into the bucket, clouds of steam wafted out. The Elder battled the sun over the right to the steam, exclaiming, *I'm already seventy-two years old. Is there anything I haven't experienced? Do you think I can be defeated by a dried-up well? As long as there is water underground, I'll figure out a way to find it. Sun, if you have the patience, you can try to dry up the water underground.*

In the end, the Elder won the battle.

One day, the Elder dug in his nephew's field continuously from dawn till dusk, but only ended up with half a bowl of corn seeds. The next day he went to another family's field, but didn't manage to find even half a bowl. Over a span of three days, the Elder and the dog had to shift from eating three times a day to eating only twice, and in place of corn soup they instead had to settle for dilute broth. The Elder realized that the situation was becoming quite desperate, but what he couldn't understand was—if each family had sowed their fields with corn seeds that never sprouted—why wasn't the soil full of seeds? Upon seeing the dog's ribs poking out, the Elder broke into a cold sweat. He touched his own cheeks, and found that he could pull his skin several inches from his face, as though his skin was but a piece of cloth draped loosely over his skull. He felt completely drained, and while hauling the quilt up from the bottom of the well he repeatedly had to stop and rest. The Elder thought, *I can't let myself starve to death like this.*

The Elder said, *Blindy, I have no choice but to scale a court-yard wall and break into someone's house.*

He added, *Let's just think of it as borrowing. I'll return every-thing after there's a harvest.*

The Elder took a sack and staggered back to the village. The dog silently followed him. The Elder curled his toes, so that he was walking on his heels and the tips of his toes, while keeping the arches of his feet elevated so as not to touch the hot ground. The blind dog, meanwhile, would stop every few steps and lick its paws. It seemed as though it took the two of them a year to make it to the village, and when they finally reached a cattle pen near the front of the village, the Elder huddled in the wall's shadow, removed his shoes, and massaged his feet.

The dog also sat in the shade, panting, then peed a drop of urine against the wall.

The Elder said, *Let's borrow some grain from this household.* He removed an axe from his sack and proceeded to smash open the lock on the front entrance. Then he pushed the door open and went inside. He went directly to the doorway lead-ing to the main room, and smashed that lock as well. When he stepped into the main room, he saw that the table was covered with a thick layer of dust, and there were cobwebs everywhere. Between the dust and the cobwebs, there was a memorial tablet, and a portrait of an old man. The figure in the picture was wearing a robe and a mandarin jacket. He had bright eyes that cut through the dust, and his gaze seemed to come to rest on the Elder.

The Elder stared in shock.

This was old Baozhang's house. Old Baozhang had died only three years earlier, and his gaze still appeared sharp and lively. The Elder wondered, *Blindy, are you really blind? How did you know to pee at the entrance of Baozhang's home?* He leaned his axe against the doorway, knelt down and kowtowed three times, then bowed three more times. He said, *Baozhang, the Balou Mountains are several hundred li wide, but now the entire region is in the grip of a once-in-a-millennium drought. All the other residents—including men and women, young and old—have fled, and Blindy and I are the only ones left in the village, or even the entire world. We stayed behind to look after the village, but it has been three days since we had a real meal. Today, we have come to your house to borrow some food, but next year we will definitely return everything. Furthermore, Baozhang, you need not mind us—I already know where each family hid the grain they kept in reserve in case of drought.* Upon saying this, the Elder got up, dusted the dirt from his knees, then carried his grain sack into one of the inner rooms, where he looked in all of the jugs and jars. They were completely empty, but the Elder was not discouraged. It seemed as though he knew that the family's grain wouldn't be stored in such an obvious place. Next, he looked under the bed. Using the light that was coming in through the window, he carefully inspected the area beneath the bed in the eastern room, and thought, *When everyone fled the famine, would they have left their grain in the open for thieves to find? If it were me, I would have hidden mine under my bed.* But, other than a porcelain urine basin, the area under Baozhang's bed was completely empty, without even a speck of dirt. The Elder then moved the empty jugs and jars out of the way, to look under the table and inside the cabinet. The sound of him moving things around echoed through the three-room house. He rummaged about for a long time, until he was covered in dust and cobwebs, but still couldn't manage to find a single grain of wheat.

The Elder dusted off his hands and said, *Baozhang. Ah, Baozhang. When you were still alive, I never did you wrong, and even though I'm six months older than you, I've always called you Elder Brother. If there wasn't any leftover grain in your house, you should have just said so! Instead, you've made me spend half the day looking for nothing, as though I had limitless energy—as though, if I were to leave your house, I wouldn't be able to find any grain elsewhere.*

Baozhang, of course, didn't respond.

When Baozhang didn't respond, the Elder tossed him a glance, and added, *Yes, it's true. You made me kowtow and bow to you for nothing.* Afterward, he patted the head of the blind dog, who was lying in the entranceway, and said, *Let's go. I'm sure we'll have better luck elsewhere.*

The Elder closed the door and hung up the broken lock—leaving the door the way he had found it—then proceeded to enter one house after another. He went to seven houses in a row—and each time he broke the lock on the front door, went inside, and searched their grain jars and jugs, in and around their cabinets, under their beds and tables. He searched each house with a fine comb, but in the end he was unable to find even a single speck of grain. When he emerged from the seventh house, the Elder took a food scale and a horse whip—this family had a horse-drawn carriage, and the Elder had previously helped them drive it—then he went out into the street and stood there at a loss. He dropped the scale and the whip on the side of the road, and asked himself, *Why do I need a scale? If I could find enough grain to weigh on a scale, in the future I could return the correct amount of grain to its owner, but where in the world am I going to find any grain?* He said, *What do I need a whip for? Although I could use a whip like a gun to protect myself*—the Elder had once used a whip to kill a wolf—*the animals in the mountains have all fled and now there isn't even a single rabbit left. Isn't this whip completely useless?* As the sun shone through the cracks in each door, every house was illuminated more brightly than before. The Elder glanced up at the sky, and saw that the sun was already at its zenith. It was lunchtime, but he hadn't smelled the faintest hint of grain. A feeling of desperation surged in his heart. He told the blind dog to sit down in the street, saying, *You should wait here. Since you are completely blind, you wouldn't be able to see where everyone has hidden their grain.* Then he headed over to another alley, where he selected several houses with plenty of sunlight, and broke into them. Yet even after he had entered three more residences, his grain sack remained completely empty. When he reemerged from the alley, the bright sunlight made him appear pale, and a sense of acute sorrow coursed through the deep furrows of his face. The Elder was holding a salt shaker that had half a pinch of salt inside, and he put a single grain of salt into his mouth, then went to put one into the dog's mouth as well.

The dog looked at him inquisitively with its blind eyes, seeming to ask, *Could it be that you didn't find any food?*

The Elder didn't answer. Instead, he picked up the whip, stood in the middle of the road, and began whipping the sun. The thin leather whip writhed through the air like a snake, producing a series of sharp, explosive cracks. The Elder whipped the sun until its fragments fell to the earth like pear petals, covering the ground with shattered sunlight, and the entire village seemed to be filled with the sound of New Year's fireworks. Only after the Elder was exhausted and covered in sweat, did he finally put away the whip.

Deeply disappointed, the blind dog stood in front of the Elder, as its eye sockets grew moist.

The Elder said, *Blindy, don't be afraid. In the future, whenever I have a bowl of grain, I'll give you half. I would rather starve than let you die of hunger.*

The blind dog's eyes filled with tears. The teardrops fell to the ground, creating two bean-like depressions in the earth.

Let's go. The Elder picked up the salt shaker, as well as the whip and the scale. He said, *Let's return to the hill and dig for more seeds.*

After they had only walked a couple of steps, the Elder came to an abrupt halt. He saw a swarm of rats, each of which was round and fat, as though it were a year with a bumper harvest. The rats waited under the shade of the wall, staring uneasily at the village, the Elder, and the blind dog. Suddenly, it was as if a door in the Elder's mind had swung open.

The Elder laughed.

This was the first time the Elder had laughed since the other villagers fled, and his crackling laugh was hoarse and brittle, like slow-roasted soybeans. The Elder said, *You can starve the sky and you can starve the earth, but you certainly can't starve this old man.*

The Elder led the blind dog over to the terrified rats, and said, *Blindy, do you know where all the grain is hidden? I do. I know.*

That night, the Elder dug up three rat nests and collected a *sheng* of corn seeds. The Elder spent the first half of the night sleeping lightly in the shed, then around midnight—under the stars and the bright moon, and as the ground was covered with a bright sheet of moonlight—the Elder told the dog to stand guard by the corn sprout while he went to the center of the field, where he sat down and held his breath. He stayed this way for a while, until he was able to hear rats rustling around. This was not the sound of rats playing happily, but rather they were fighting over food. The Elder pressed his ear to the ground, confirming where exactly the sounds were coming from, then used a stake to mark the spot. Next, he went back to fetch his hoe and began digging. Sure enough, three feet from the stake and one foot down, he found a rat's nest in which there was the equivalent of half a bowl of corn seeds. The Elder didn't leave a single seed behind, even scooping up the rat droppings along with the grain. Then he went to a second spot, and followed the same process.

The Elder's days were busy. In the morning he would wake and go to the village to haul the water-soaked quilt up from the well. After returning to his field and eating breakfast, he would pick out the rat droppings from the grain, and then put the grain in a bowl. After the bowl was full, he would bury it next to the corn sprout. After lunch, he would need to take a nap, and although the sun shone brightly into the shed, it wasn't as sweltering as it was outside, and sometimes a cool breeze would even blow through. He would sleep soundly, and when he woke up the sun would already be over the western mountains. He would then go back to the village to wring another half a bucket of water from the quilt, after which dusk would arrive as usual. He would have dinner and then would sit with the dog by the corn sprout in the cold fear and solitude of the night. He would ask the dog and the sprout some questions that had been troubling him, such as, *Why do crops grow one leaf at a time?* Neither the dog nor the sprout was able to offer an answer, so the Elder simply lit his pipe, took a long drag, and said, *Let me tell you. It's because they are crops, which is why they have to grow one leaf at a time. And because others are plants, they grow two leaves at a time.* Some nights, the wind would blow as usual, and the Elder would ask the dog and the sprout even more profound questions, such as, *You knew? When old Baozhang was still alive, a scholar once came to the village and said that this earth was spinning around, and each time it spun around once, this was a day. You tell me, wasn't this scholar simply farting in the wind? If the earth were spinning, then why aren't we knocked out of our beds when we sleep in the village at night? Why does water not spill out of the water jugs, or stream out of wells? Why do people always walk with their heads pointed toward the sky?* The Elder added, *Based on what that man said, the earth must be sucking us in, so that we don't fall out of our beds at night. But just think, if the earth were sucking us in, then how would we be able to lift our feet when we walk?* As the Elder was discussing these sorts of questions, which were as deep and murky as a dark hole, he would stop smoking his pipe and assume a very solemn expression. Finally, he laid out all of his questions in front of the dog and the sprout, then fell to the ground, such that his face was now parallel with the sky. He let the moonlight wash over him, and said, *I was too polite to that scholar, and was too concerned with trying not to make him lose face. He stayed in the village for three days, but I didn't ask him about any of this. I was afraid that if he were unable to answer my questions, he might lose face in front of the entire village.* The Elder added, *To eat and survive, that scholar relied on his learning, which I couldn't bring myself to shatter.*

The cornstalk continued growing smoothly. Its leaves were now as wide as a man's palm, extending layer after layer from the ground up to the reed mats, and beyond. By now the stalk was already twice as high as the mats, and the sound of it growing at night had become a dull roar. In a few more days, the stalk would reach its full height. In order to make it easier to enter the enclosure, the Elder cut open one of the mats. Seven days earlier he had gone in to compare his height with that of the stalk, and found that the stalk already reached his neck, and two days later it was up to his forehead. Within half a month, the stalk should start producing ears, and after three months the corn should be ripe. The Elder thought about how, in this barren and desolate mountain range, he would have succeeded in growing an ear of corn, and how he would collect a bowlful of corn, with each grain being as precious as a pearl. Eventually, the rains would finally come, the villagers would return to the village, and they would be able to use this bowl of corn seeds for sowing. In this way, the mountain range could once again be covered in endless fields of green corn. The Elder thought, *After I die, they should erect a plaque reading* BOUNDLESS BENEFICENCE *in front of my grave.*

The Elder continued talking to himself, saying, *I am indeed full of beneficence,* and as he was saying this, he slipped into a dream. Later, still asleep, he climbed down from his shed, went over to the cornstalk, and hoed around it. In the quiet night, the rhythmic and resonant sound of his hoeing was like a melodic line in a folk music performance. Throughout the mountain range, the sound spread far and wide. After he finished hoeing, the Elder didn't return to bed, and instead he took his hoe to another location, where he again held his breath to listen for signs of a rat's nest filled with corn seeds. When he woke up the next morning, he discovered that his bowl, which had been empty, was now full of corn and rat droppings. He stood next to the bowl for a long time, staring in shock.

There was a grain sack hanging from one of the shed posts, and it was already half full of corn. Three days earlier, at around noon, the Elder had been sleeping and the blind dog had run over and tugged at him until he woke up. The dog then dragged him out to the corner of a field located several dozen steps away. When they arrived, the Elder discovered a rat's nest full of corn. When the Elder took the corn back and weighed it, he found that it was about four or five *qian*. So, it turned out that the blind dog could find rat nests as well. The dog would run around a field, sniffing the ground, and whenever it found a nest, it would start barking.

As his grain sack grew fat, the Elder stopped going out to the fields in the middle of the night to find rat nests. Instead, he would take the dog, whereupon each of the nests would be revealed—though half of them actually contained no grain. The Elder and the blind dog now had a surplus of grain, and within a few days, the grain sack was filled to the brim. However, just when the Elder felt that he could sleep comfortably and was able to forget about having to frantically dig up all of the rat nests on the ridge, it turned out that the rats had stopped digging up the corn seeds and taking them back to their nests for storage, and instead had begun competing with the Elder to see who could consume their stored grain the fastest. One day—when the sun appeared much nearer than it had in the past and the soil along the mountain ridge had become like a burning-red iron plate—the Elder couldn't sleep, and decided to weigh his grain. He took his scale, and when he weighed the grain in the shade, it came out to one *liang,* but when he took it into the sunlight, the scale instead read 1.2 *liang.* The Elder was startled. He took the scale up to the hill, where the sun was shining even brighter, and there the scale read 1.25 *liang.*

Astonished, the Elder found that when the sun was shining brightly, its weight could register on the scale. The Elder ran up to the mountain ridge, and found that at the top of the ridge the scale read 1.31 *liang.* After subtracting the one-*liang* weight of the plate itself, that meant the sunlight weighed 0.31 *liang,* which is to say 3.1 *qian.* The Elder quickly climbed four more mountain ridges, each taller than the last, and found that at the top of the tallest ridge the sunlight weighed 5.3 *qian.*

From this point on, the Elder repeatedly weighed the sunlight. When the sun first came out in the morning, the sunlight around the shed weighed two *qian,* by midday it had increased to four *qian,* and at sunset it had reverted back to two *qian.*

The Elder also weighed his rice bowl and water bucket. Once, as he was weighing the blind dog's ear, the dog knocked the scale's balance arm and struck his face, so he hit the dog in the head.

By the time the Elder decided to weigh the corn seeds again, he had already been weighing the sunlight for four days, and had eaten several servings of corn. When he added up the weight of all the corn, the Elder stared in shock. It turned out that the remainder would only last him and the blind dog for another half a month, at most. It was then that it occurred to him that it had been several days since he and the blind dog had gone out to the fields to look for rat nests.

It was already too late! In just a few days, the rats, as though they had received advance notice, had consumed all of the grain they had stored up in their nests. The Elder spent an entire afternoon leading the blind dog to seven different hillside fields, where the two of them dug up thirty-one rat nests. They worked until they were about to drop, but only managed to dig up eight *liang* of corn. At sunset, the sun's blood-colored light shone down from the western mountains onto the ridge, the corn leaves that had been curled up during the day finally began to uncurl and exhale. The Elder brought over that half-bowl of corn mixed with rat droppings, and it suddenly occurred to him that the rats up on the ridge were now competing with him and the blind dog for grain.

The Elder wondered, *Where have they taken all of their grain?*

He thought, *No matter how clever they may be, they'll never be able to outsmart me.*

That night, the Elder and the blind dog went to listen for rats in an even more distant field. They visited three different fields that night, but didn't hear a sound. Just as the eastern sky was beginning to lighten, the Elder returned with the dog, and he asked, *Have the rats moved away? If so, where did they go? Wherever they went, there must be grain, so we have to find them.* The sunlight shone down on the dog's empty eye sockets. The dog cocked its head and walked away with its back to the sun without hearing what the Elder was saying.

The Elder asked, *Could the rats be hiding somewhere, to compete with us?*

The dog paused, then turned and followed the sound of the Elder's footsteps.

When they arrived at the shed, the Elder went to inspect the cornstalk, and found that the stem was now as wide as a child's wrist. Then he prepared to return to the village to fetch some water. He collected two empty buckets, and wanted to take the dog along with him. The dog, however, was lying motionless under the shed. The Elder said, *Let's go. Let's go to the village and see which houses have rats in them, so that we can know where to look for grain.* Only then did the dog get up and accompany him. In the village, apart from two rats that had drowned in the well, they didn't see a single rodent in the streets, alleyways, or the entranceways of the houses whose doors they had pried open. When the Elder returned to Baliban

Hill with his load of water, he discovered that everything was in disarray. When they were half a *li* from the hillside field, the dog began to act ill at ease, and periodically barked a purplish yelp. The Elder quickened his pace. He climbed the ridge, and when the field appeared before him, the dog suddenly stopped barking and instead began running like crazy toward their shed. In the process it almost fell off the cliff. The hard sunlight on the ground was shattered by the dog's footsteps, producing an explosive sound like a bottle shattering, and its sharp, frantic barks saturated the fields like red blood.

The Elder stared in shock.

The Elder was standing at the far end of the field, and in the intervals between the dog's barks, he could hear the squeaking of rats, like drizzling rain. Then, he went to the shed in the middle of the field and saw that the grain sack he had hung on one of the poles had fallen. Its contents had spilled onto the hardened ground. A black mass of rats—numbering three to five hundred, or perhaps even a thousand or more— were fighting over the spilled corn seeds. They were running back and forth, and the seeds rolled around under their feet and dribbled out of their mouths. The sound of them chewing mingled with their excited laughter, and the sound rained down on the hillside like a thunderstorm. The Elder stood there speechless, as the dog ran over and bumped its head on one of the poles. Blood spurted into the air, whereupon the dog and the rats fell into a stupor. After a moment they came to their senses, and the dog once again began running around barking, becoming so frantic that it hit one of the posts with its paw. The rats didn't realize the dog was blind, and were so terrified by its frenzy that they began crying darkly. The result was a cacophony of cursing and terror, as the mountain ridge, which had been deathly quiet for the past two months, suddenly began to boil over. As the Elder ran through the mass of rats, he stepped on one and heard a scream, as hot blood splattered over his other foot. The Elder ran to the enclosure and dove inside, and as he feared, there were two thirsty rats eating that watery-green cornstalk. When the rats heard the Elder barge in, they paused and then ran out through an opening in the side of the enclosure. Upon seeing that the cornstalk was standing there intact, the Elder relaxed. He turned and left the enclosure, and saw that several starving rats were still scurrying around in the grain sack under the shed. He grabbed the hoe leaning against the mats and used it to hit the sack, whereupon a multitude of red droplets spurted out. He struck the sack several times in a row, as rat fur flew everywhere and the ground became splattered with blood. The remaining several dozen rats shrieked in terror and shot out in all directions, disappearing in the blink of an eye.

The blind dog stopped barking.

The Elder leaned against his hoe, breathing heavily.

The Balou Mountains suddenly became very silent—a thick and heavy silence that was several times more ponderous than it had been in the past. The Elder guessed that hundreds and thousands of rats must be hiding nearby, and would come rushing back as soon as he left. He glanced at the mountains around him, then sat down on the hoe handle and picked up the corn seeds that had spilled. He said, *Blindy, what are we going to do? Can you guard this?* The blind dog lay on the ground that had been warmed by the sunlight and stuck out its tongue. The Elder said, *I don't have any water. I, you, and the cornstalk—none of us has a single drop to drink.*

The Elder didn't cook any food that day. He and the blind dog went hungry, and after nightfall they stood guard by the enclosure around the cornstalk. They were afraid it would take a couple of rats just a few bites to gnaw through the stalk, so they kept watch until dawn. In the end, they didn't see any rats. Around noon the following day, the Elder noticed that one of the leaves had begun to curl in the sunlight, and only then did he go fetch a pair of empty buckets.

The Elder said, *Blindy, I want you to stand guard by the cornstalk.*

The Elder said, *You can lie in the shade, and keep your ear to the ground. If you hear even the faintest sound, then bark loudly in that direction.*

The Elder said, *I'm going to go fetch some water, and you must stay alert.*

When the Elder returned with half a bucket of water, everything appeared to be all right. The only problem was that when he had hauled the quilt out of the well, he found that it contained four drowned rats whose soaked fur was full of fleas. The Elder ate his meal, then placed the corn seeds on a couple of stones. As he was grinding the seeds, he began to feel anxious. His corn reserve had been devoured by the rats to the point that he now had only half a sack left. The Elder weighed the remainder, and found that he still had six *jin* and two *liang*. If he consumed only half a portion for each meal, three times a day, then he and the dog would consume one *jin* each day. What would they do in six days, after their provisions were exhausted?

The sun was about to set, and the mountain ridge to the west was drenched in a bloody red aura. The Elder gazed at the myriad colors under this sheet of red, and it occurred to him that he would soon use up their food, and would run out of water two or three days later. He looked at the cornstalk, and saw that the top had begun to turn pink. He tried to calculate how long it would be until it started producing tassel, and how long until it produced an ear. It occurred to him that many, many days had already passed, and he could no longer remember what day or even what month it was. He noticed that apart from not knowing whether it was day or night, morning or dusk, sunrise or moonset—these sorts of time periods that occur each day—he had even lost all awareness of time. His mind was a complete blank. He said, *Blindy, have we already passed the first day of autumn?* But he didn't look at the dog, and instead merely mumbled to himself, *For all we know, we've already entered the following solar term, and it's generally around this time that corn begins producing tassel.*

The Elder squinted, and proceeded to grind the corn seeds on the stone's surface. He watched as the blind dog sniffed the ground, then picked up a dead rat and carried it over to the gully. When the dog was several feet from the edge of the gully, it shook its head and tossed the rat in.

The Elder noticed a faint stench.

The dog returned and grabbed another dead rat, then took it to the edge of the gully as well.

The Years, Months, Days

The Elder needed a calendar. He stared at the dog, and it occurred to him that without a calendar, there were no dates; and with no dates, he had no way of knowing when the corn would ripen. There were perhaps still thirty or forty days until the autumn harvest. But what would he eat during this intervening period? The rats had consumed all of the seeds in the fields. The Elder raised his head and heard shrill screams coming from the west. He peered into the distance, and between the two mountain peaks he could see the sun being swallowed by another mountain peak. The remaining blood-red stain flowed from the peaks down to the foot of the mountains, then back up to the Elder. The entire world became completely silent. It was once again the quietest time of day, between dusk and nightfall. In the past, this would be when chickens returned to roost and sparrows went back to their nests, and the entire world would be filled with rain-like chirping. But now there wasn't a sound. There were no live-stock, no sparrows, and even the crows had fled the drought. There was only silence. The Elder saw that the setting sun's bloodlike glow was becoming fainter and fainter, and he listened as it was blown farther away from him, like a sheet of silk. He collected the ground-up seeds from the stone and thought, *Another day has ended, but how will I endure tomorrow, when the sun is again overhead?*

Three more days elapsed, and no matter how hard he tried to economize, he still used up more than half of the remaining corn. The Elder wondered, *Where have all the rats gone? What are they living on?*

On the fourth night, he summoned the blind dog over to the cornstalk, and said, *I want you to keep watch, and if you hear any movement, just bark.* Then, the Elder grabbed a hoe and headed north up the mountain ridge. When he reached a field located farthest from the village, he placed his hoe in the middle of the field, then sat down on the handle. He sat there until the dawn light was visible in the east, but didn't hear a sound. The next day he led the blind dog out to this field, and the dog helped him find seven rat nests. After he dug up the nests, however, he discovered that inside there were no rats or grain, and apart from some droppings the only thing he found was hot, rocky soil. He searched for the hoe marks from when the field's owner originally sowed the corn, then dug several new holes—but still didn't find any seeds.

It finally struck him that in this entire mountain ridge there wasn't a single speck of food left.

Blindy, the Elder said, *What do you think? Are we going to starve to death?*

The blind dog stared into the sky with its eyes that were as dark as the bottom of a well.

The Elder said, *I don't think the stalk will ever mature.*

They entered the fifth night, and as soon as the sun set, darkness arrived with a crackling sound. The entire mountainside was covered in moonless and starless darkness. At this point, the desiccated old trees on the mountainside had just received some moisture, and they quickly let out a delicate sigh. The Elder sat down with his dog next to the cornstalk, and scratched his nose with one of the leaves. He inhaled several gulps of fragrant air, whereupon the scent of grain rushed toward his intestines like a horse-drawn carriage careening down the street. He waited until the odor reached his belly, then he clinched his abdomen, trapping the odor inside his stomach. As he was doing this, he heard the faint sound of moonlight falling to earth, and said, *Blindy, you should come over and have a few bites. That way you won't be hungry.* He called to the animal a couple of times, but didn't see any movement. When he turned, he saw that the dog was lying on a mat like a pile of mud. He reached over to touch it, then jumped back in alarm. The dog's stomach was poking through its skin, so sharp that it cut his hand like a knife. The Elder then felt his own stomach. He first peeled off a layer of cracked, dirty skin and tossed it to the ground, then he touched the soft skin beneath it, and found that he could feel his lower vertebrae poking through from his back.

Blindy, the Elder said, *look, the moon has emerged. You should sleep, because if you do you won't be hungry. You can treat your dreams as though they were food.*

The dog stood up and staggered to the shed.

Don't climb onto the shed, the Elder said. *Just sleep on the ground. That way you can save your energy.*

The dog returned to where it had originally been lying, and stopped moving.

The crescent moon slowly emerged from behind a cloud, and the mountain ridge appeared as though it were covered in water. In the haze, the Elder stared into the dark night, and prayed, *Am I about to starve to death? Please give me some grain, so that I may survive a few more days. At the very least, I want to outlive the dog, so that after it dies I can pick a good spot and bury it. That way the rats won't be able to devour its corpse, and won't be able to prevent it from returning to the mortal world in the next life. After the dog dies, please let me survive to watch this cornstalk. After the corn is ripe, don't let me die. I must make it until the next rainfall—until the villagers return to the ridge, so that I can give them this ear of corn. This corn belongs to the mountain ridge.* As the Elder was praying, he caressed a corn leaf with one hand, while continuing to peel off some dead skin from his stomach. As the Elder was about to go to sleep, he gently placed his feet on the dog's back, and said, *Go to sleep, Blindy. After you fall asleep, you'll forget your hunger.* With this, the Elder's eyelids slammed shut and he staggered off into dreamland.

As the Elder was sleeping, he kicked his feet that had been resting on the dog's back, and the dog's barking shattered his sleep like a stone. The Elder sat up and heard the faint sound of rats squeaking on the ridge, and the sound of their tiny paws. The dog was standing outside of the reed mats, barking in the direction of the mountain ridge. The Elder patted the dog's head and told it to go back inside the enclosure to guard the cornstalk. This happened just as the sun was about to rise, the moonlight was beginning to fade, and the air had a faint scent of moisture. The Elder climbed onto the shed and squatted down on the side facing the mountain ridge. He noticed there was a strong, dark-red rat stench, and there was also dust flying everywhere. He blinked his eyes, but all he could see was a cloud-like mass over the mountain road, rapidly moving south. He climbed back down off the shed, afraid that the swarm of rats would suddenly turn around and begin rushing toward the stalk. He looked at the enclosure, and saw that the stalk was still standing straight. The blind dog's ears perked up, and the Elder patted its head and said, *You mustn't bark. You mustn't remind the rats we are here. They know that wherever there are people, there will also be food.*

At that point, the roar on the mountain ridge, which sounded like an approaching thunderstorm, suddenly died down. The Elder patted the dog's head again, then quietly made his way toward the ridge. When he arrived, he saw that a steady stream of rats, in groups of ten or twenty, were breaking rank and, squeaking loudly, were heading south. He couldn't believe his eyes—the road, which had previously been as hard as an iron plate, was now covered in a finger-thick layer of dust. The rats' paw prints piled on top of one another, to the point that there wasn't enough empty space between them to insert a needle.

The Elder stood by the road, staring in shock.

The Elder thought, *Where could they all be going?*

Perhaps this drought will continue indefinitely. The Elder thought, *If the drought wasn't going to last, why would the rats flee? Isn't it true that the rats will always have vegetation to eat, and the only thing they fear is lack of water? Given that the rats are fleeing, it's obvious that the drought is going to persist for a lot longer.* But when the Elder turned to leave, he once again heard the sound of rain coming from the north. He knew, however, that this was not in fact rain, but rather another swarm of rats. He shuddered, then stood on an elevated point and gazed out into the distance. As he did, the blood suddenly froze in his veins. He saw that what was streaming down the mountain appeared to be a wall of water surging along the road, but in fact it was a flood-like mass of shrieking rats. The wave of rats rose and fell, and as they approached, their sound changed from that of a drizzle to a torrential downpour. Countless rats leaped up like fish jumping out of water, then fell back into the sea of rodents. The sky was already beginning to brighten, and the air was filled with a foul stench. The Elder's palms became covered in sweat, and he knew that if this wave of rats were to turn around, then he, the blind dog, and the cornstalk would be doomed. The rats were crazed with hunger, and were capable of chewing a man's face off. The Elder wanted to run back and tell the blind dog that it mustn't move a muscle, but it was already too late. Like a dark cloud, the wave of rats surged forward. The Elder hid under the branches of a pagoda tree, though the tree was only as thick as his arm. Several rats at the front were enormous—as large as weasels or small cats—and were covered in shimmering gray fur. The Elder had never seen such large rats, and it occurred to him that these must be what people used to call rat kings. He saw that those rats had bright green eyes that sparkled with a bright blue light. They leaped forward like horses, and with each leap they could travel at least a foot and a half. The dust they kicked up covered their backs like gray felt. The Elder squeezed his throat to stifle a sneeze. The sky was growing light, and the cool dawn was approaching as usual. Snow-white clouds were drifting across the bright blue sky, but the sun was brighter than ever. If it weren't, would these rats be fleeing like this? The Elder slipped out from behind the tree, but not a single rat was willing to look straight at him. They seemed to view him as no longer human, but rather an extension of the sky, the sun, or the searing drought. The

Elder stood there motionless watching the rats rush past, and could hear them falling off the road, like ripe persimmons. What he couldn't understand was how were the rats able to come together to form such an enormous pile? They seemed to be under orders to march south, but what was in the south? Was there grain and water and shade? To the east there was the golden sun, and the Elder suddenly noticed that the rats' eyes had all turned bright red, and appeared to roll down the street like a wave of pearls. Hundreds and thousands of rats that had been pushed off the road began running through the fields on either side, only to disappear in the blink of an eye.

The sun came out, and strand after strand of fur fluttered in the sunlight, like willow catkins and poplar blossoms. The Elder stood on the ridge and sighed, then proceeded back down. His footsteps echoed softly in the morning air, sounding old and listless. When he reached the cornstalk, he saw that the blind dog was staring at the mountain ridge with its blind eyes, as sweat dripped from the tips of its ears.

The Elder asked, *What are you afraid of?*

The dog didn't respond, and instead it simply lay down beside him.

The Elder asked, *Are you afraid there will be a catastrophe?*

The dog still didn't answer, and instead it simply looked at the cornstalk.

The Elder stared in surprise, noticing that on the stalk's leaves there were countless white dots, like sesame seeds. These were the sorts of dry patches that usually only appear during periods of prolonged drought. However, despite the current drought, this stalk had never lacked water. The Elder had dug an irrigation moat around the stalk, to which he had added water virtually every day. He squatted down and lifted the dirt in the moat, and found that under a finger-thick layer of dry soil there was another layer of dirt so wet you could virtually pick up water droplets with your fingers. The Elder grabbed a fistful of this wet soil and realized that those dry patches were a result not of the drought, but rather of the rat stench that pervaded the entire mountainside.

Of all manure, rat excrement is the strongest and the most pungent, the Elder thought. *Given that this stench has surrounded the stalk all night, how could the stalk have possibly avoided developing dry patches?* He pressed his ear to the leaves, and found he could hear the squeaking sound made by the dry patches as they expanded. When he turned to smell the air, he noticed a wave of dark, dry rat stench wafting over—flowing toward the cornstalk like a river.

That is to say, the stalk was about to die.

If the stalk hoped to survive, there would need to be a sudden downpour that would wash away this poisonous stench covering the entire mountainside, and wash away the poisonous air from the stalk itself.

The blind dog sensed the Elder's alarm. The Elder said, *Blindy, you should stand guard while I return to the village to fetch some water.* Not waiting to see if the dog was going to respond, the Elder picked up the empty buckets and headed into the village.

By this point, the village was completely silent. There was a layer of rat excrement by the side of the road, and an unrelenting sun shone through the cracks in the front door of each house. The Elder headed straight for the well. As he was hauling up the quilt from the bottom of the well, he noticed that the rope was so light it seemed as though there was nothing there; and whereas in the past he would hear the sound of water dripping down, now there was nothing. The Elder peered inside, and turned white as a sheet.

After a long pause, the Elder finally hauled up the remainder of the rope. The quilt was no longer tied to the other end, and instead all that remained was a layer of damaged cloth covered with bloated rat carcasses.

The quilt had been devoured by starving rats that had fallen into the well.

The Elder went into someone's house to look for another quilt or some sheets.

The Elder first went to the houses where he had previously searched for grain, but each time he arrived at a house he would merely pause in the doorway. The entire village had been swept clean by the rats. In every house, the chests, tables, cabinets, beds, and so forth—everything that had previously contained clothing or food—had been chewed up like a bowl of sunflower seeds. A delicate mix of wood odor and rat stench filled each room and drifted into the courtyard.

The Elder entered more than ten houses, but emerged from each empty-handed.

When he walked out through the village alleyway, the Elder was carrying three bamboo poles. He tied the poles together, then went to an outhouse in the rear courtyard of another house and fetched a wooden bowl used to scoop excrement—every family's stove bellows, chopping boards, wooden bowls, and pottery bowls had been completely gnawed by the rats—and he tied it to the end of the bamboo poles. He then dipped the bowl three times into the well to get water, but all he brought up were more rats. Using the sunlight shining overhead, the Elder peered into the well, and he saw that there was in fact no water at the bottom. Instead, the bottom of the well was covered in a pile of rats, like a storage cellar full of rotten sweet potatoes. There were also some live rats running over the bodies of the dead ones. The live rats would climb a few feet up the sides of the well then fall down again, as their anguished squeals rose through the shaft.

The Elder carried the empty buckets back to Baliban Hill.

The mountain range stretched endlessly in all directions. Dozens of *li* away, where the mountains touched the horizon, it appeared as though there were fires burning brightly. When the Elder reached the hill, the blind dog ran over. The Elder reported that the well was completely dry, and full of rats. He asked the dog whether there were any rats here, but the dog shook its head. The Elder said, *You and I will be killed by the rats, as will the cornstalk. We won't survive more than a few days.*

Disappointed, the dog stood in the shade of the shed, staring at the sky.

After putting down his bucket, the Elder went inside the enclosure to take a look, and found that each of the dry spots on the leaves was now as large as a fingernail. For what seemed like an eternity, the Elder stood silently in front of the stalk, staring as dry spots on the eleventh leaf expanded and merged together until the leaf came to resemble a dried-out bean pod. He blinked his sleepy eyes, and blue veins protruded from his neck like old roots sticking out of the ground. He left the enclosure, grabbed a whip from the shed, and aimed it at the center of the sun, then whipped the sun more than a dozen times—producing a multitude of shimmering shadows. Eventually, the veins in his neck receded, and he hung the whip back where he had found it, fetched the buckets, and proceeded silently up the ridge.

The dog faced the Elder, its melancholy black eyes full of tears. When the Elder's footsteps faded away, the dog finally turned away, lying down in the sunlight under the cornstalk.

The Elder had gone to fetch water.

The Elder realized that the swarm of rats must be coming from a place where there was water, otherwise how could the rats have survived the drought for so long? The Elder thought, *It must be a lack of food that is driving them to flee, because if there had been food, why would they have devoured all of the woodwork in the village?* The Elder thought, *This mass exodus must not be due to a lack of water.* The sun's rays were bright red, and as the Elder walked alone through the mountain ridge, he could count every ray as it streaked past. The pair of buckets dangling from his shoulder pole knocked plaintively against each other, as the soil under his feet seemed to be sighing. The Elder heard this knocking and sighing, and felt a sense of desolation that seemed vaster than all of the world's drought-plagued land. He visited three villages in a row, and found that in each of them the dried-up wells were full of grass and straw, without even a hint of mold or rot. The Elder decided not to go into the villages to seek water—because if there had been water, then why would the villagers have fled in the first place? Instead, he proceeded from one gully to another, searching for any trace of moisture. Finally, he was walking through a narrow ridge when he noticed some thatch grass growing in the shade of the stone. He exclaimed, *Fuck, how could there not be a way forward?* Then he sat down on the stone to rest, and proceeded to pull up some grass, blade by blade. He sucked out the juice and swallowed the chewed-up remains. He said to himself, *If this ravine doesn't have any water either, I'm definitely going to bash my head in.*

He proceeded toward the ravine, breathing heavily, as though winter had suddenly fallen in front of him. He wasn't sure how far he had walked. When he was chewing the grass, the reddish-white sun was still hanging over the mountain ridge to the west, but now he noticed that the cracked earth under his feet had been replaced by white sand and the sun appeared blood red.

By the time the Elder found a tiny spring, it was already dusk. He first noticed that the white sand under his feet had turned light red from the humidity, and his feet, which were burning hot from walking all day, suddenly enjoyed a trace of coolness. Walking on the wet sand, the Elder proceeded into the ravine, and when it became so narrow that it felt as though it were pressed against his shoulders, the sound of dripping water streamed over him, like music. The Elder looked up, and saw a sheet of green heading toward him. The Elder stopped. He had not seen this much grass in more than five months, and had almost forgotten what it looked like. There was sedge grass and thatch grass, and also small white, red, and reddish-white flowers. Under the searing sun, a strong scent of fresh vegetation rolled noisily through the ravine. The Elder's throat began to tighten, and an irresistible thirst arrived at his cracked lips. He saw that a few steps in front of him, under the cliff, there was a spring and a small pool. The pool was partially covering that small plot of grass, as if the grass were growing out from under a mirror.

Just as the Elder was about to drop his buckets and run over to drink from the pool, he paused. He repeatedly swallowed a mouthful of phlegm as he stood there without moving. He saw that behind the mound of grass there was a wolf—a yellow wolf as large as the blind dog. The wolf had bright green eyes and initially seemed surprised by the Elder's appearance, but when it realized he was carrying a pair of buckets, its gaze became fierce and its forelegs stiffened as though it were ready to pounce.

The Elder stood there motionless, staring intently. He knew that this pool was the reason the wolf had not run away. The Elder discretely looked down, and saw that on the ground next to the bucket there was a mess of fur and feathers. Suddenly realizing that the wolf must have been hiding by the pool waiting for other creatures to come drink, the Elder shuddered with terror. Seeing how emaciated the wolf was, he figured it must have been waiting there for several days. The Elder saw that there was a blood stain on the sand a couple of paces away, as well as quite a few rat heads and other remains. It was only then that he noticed the sharp, fresh stench of rotting meat. The Elder's palms became sweaty and his legs grew weak, as the wolf took a step toward him. At that instant, however, the Elder leaned over, placed the buckets on the ground, and swung his shoulder pole through the air, aiming for the wolf's head.

The wolf took a step back, as the fury in its eyes seemed to overflow and tumble to the ground.

The Elder continued to stare at the wolf.

The wolf also stared at the Elder.

Their gazes collided. In the desolate gorge, the crackling sound of their bright gazes echoed back and forth, and the sound of dripping water resonated explosively around them. The sun was about to set behind the mountains, and time rushed past their interlocked gazes like a herd of horses. The blood-red glow on the cliff in front of them began to fade, as cool air began to descend down the mountain. At some point, the Elder's forehead became covered in sweat, and a feeling of exhaustion rose up from his feet, gradually expanding as it progressed upward from his calves to his thighs. He knew he could not continue like this. He had been walking all day, while the wolf had simply been lying here waiting. He hadn't had anything to drink all day, but the wolf could drink from the spring at any time. He furtively licked his dry lips, which felt as jagged as a bed of thorns. He thought, *Can this wolf possibly drink all of this water?* Then he said out loud, *Hey, if you let me have some water, I'll make you a bowl of corn paste soup.* As the Elder was saying this, he gripped his pole tighter and tighter. The pole was aimed at the wolf's head, and even the hooks tied to each end of the carrying pole remained frozen in place.

The wolf's eyes gradually dimmed. The wolf closed its eyes, but immediately opened them again. The Elder saw that there was a hint of moisture in its hard gaze.

The Elder heard the sound of the setting sun drift over the mountains like a falling leaf. The Elder put down the pole he was holding, placing it on a clump of grass.

The Elder said, *Tomorrow I will bring you a bowl of food.*

The wolf pulled back its front paws, then turned and slowly circled around the edge of the pond, heading toward the opening of the gully. After taking several steps, the wolf stopped and looked back. The Elder watched until the wolf was several dozen paces away, before he finally released his grip and let the pole fall to the ground. He collapsed to a squatting position and shivered violently as he wiped the sweat from his forehead, and it was only then that he realized that even his underwear, which was the only thing he was wearing, was soaked in sweat.

After a long sigh, the Elder found that he lacked the strength to stand. He continued squatting there until finally he scooted forward to the side of the pool, where he lay down and drank from it like an ox. In the blink of an eye, the cool water entered through his mouth and permeated down to the soles of his feet. He drank until his belly was full, then washed his face. Seeing that the red sunlight at the top of the cliff was as thin as a sheet of paper, he picked up the bucket of water and placed it next to the pool, then removed his underwear.

The Elder bathed himself next to the pool.

While bathing, the Elder said, *Wolf, ah wolf, today you let me have some water, but tomorrow where am I going to find you a bowl of corn? I'll catch you a few rats, because I know you like* to eat meat. The Elder thought, *I'm old and weak, and therefore have no choice but to accede to you. However, if this were a decade ago, or even just a few years ago, not only would I not give you any rats to eat, it would be the ultimate act of compassion and mercy for me to simply permit you to pass under my carrying pole.* As the Elder mumbled, he continued washing himself until the clear pool was completely muddy. Then he urinated next to the pool, as the thin layer of sunlight on the top of the cliff gradually dissipated.

After picking two clumps of grass and scattering them over the water in the buckets, the Elder began slowly walking toward the opening of the gully. The buckets tugged the ends of the carrying pole until it was bent like a bow. The pole shuddered every time he took a step, but the grass he had placed in the buckets kept the water from spilling out. The pole produced a moaning sound that echoed through the gully. The Elder thought, *I really am old and should walk slowly. As long as I can make it up to the ridge before nightfall, I will have nothing to fear. The moonlight can escort me back to the hill, and after I pour the water on the cornstalk, the dry spots on its leaves will stop expanding.*

What the Elder hadn't anticipated was that a pack of wolves had already trapped him in the gully.

The original wolf was now in front, leading the way, and when the wolves saw the Elder emerging from the gully, they stopped for a moment. As the wolves were standing there, the lead wolf glanced back, then fearlessly led the others in the direction of the Elder.

The Elder's body exploded in terror, as he realized he had fallen into a trap. He thought, *If only I hadn't taken that bath.* He thought, *If only I hadn't sat down by the side of the pool to rest.* He thought, *If only I had hurried, I would be up on the ridge by now, and the wolves would have had to go away empty-handed.* He nevertheless remained calm. He carefully placed his buckets on the ground and slowly unlatched the carrying pole, then, still holding the pole, headed straight toward the pack of wolves as though he hadn't even seen them. He walked deliberately, and the carrying pole's hooks swung rhythmically back and forth. The wolves approached him, but he continued walking in their direction. The twenty-odd paces that separated them were cut to a dozen, but the Elder calmly continued forward as though he intended to march right into the wolf pack.

The wolves were disconcerted by the Elder's calmness, and they stood motionless in the opening of the gully.

The Elder continued walking straight ahead.

The two wolves at the front of the pack took a couple of steps backward, and as they did so the Elder regained a bit of confidence. He began walking quickly and vigorously, his footsteps so loud that the sound knocked some sand and pebbles down from the side of the cliff. The wolves stared at him, as the Elder proceeded to a part of the gully that was narrow like the opening of a bottle, where he squinted up at the cliff walls on either side. He selected this narrow area to make his stand. He knew the wolves would not be able to come through here, and neither would they be able to circle around and surround him.

The Elder and the wolves faced one another.

The Elder thought, *I just need to stand here and make sure I don't topple over. If I manage this, I may be able to survive long enough to make it out alive.* The sun's final rays disappeared and as night fell, the color of the gully became identical to that of the wolves' fur. In the quiet dusk, a tiny sound began to rise from the bottom of the gully. The Elder counted nine wolves in all, including three large ones, four that were about the same size as the blind dog, and two that appeared to be cubs.

The Elder stood as motionless as a tree.

The wolves' glittering green eyes appeared to be suspended in midair. The deathly silence pressed down on the Elder and the pack of wolves like the darkening mountain ridge. The Elder didn't move, nor did he make a sound. Upon realizing that the reason the Elder had been walking so quickly was to block this portion of the gully, one of the wolves began to howl, and the entire pack began advancing toward him.

The Elder planted his carrying pole in the ground in front of him.

The wolves came to a stop.

The Elder and the wolves were about seven or eight paces from one another. In the final rays of the setting sun, the Elder saw one of the three old wolves standing in the middle of the pack. Its left ear had a large chunk bitten out of it, and its leg appeared crippled. The Elder stared at the old wolf, and the two of them faced each other, until finally the wolf began to howl, at which point the entire pack once again began to advance toward the Elder, as the lead wolf fell to the back of the pack. When the wolves were still five or six paces away, the Elder waved his pole. His grip tightened as he aimed for the middle of the pack—directly at the old wolf's head.

The wolves suddenly came to a halt.

The Elder stared at the lead wolf, as the sun's dying rays swept over the pack. He noticed that the brightest eyes belonged not to the three older wolves, nor to the four midsize ones, but rather to the two cubs. Their gazes were piercingly bright, resembling a layer of water under the sunlight—though beneath this sunlit water there was a layer of fear and confusion. The other wolves kept turning around to look at the lead wolf, who produced a series of bright roars that only they could understand. The setting sun's final rays disappeared, as a sheet of darkness fell over the wolves. In the dark, the wolves' eyes shimmered like light in a blue pond. A foul odor surged through the opening of the gully. This stench was different from the sticky rat stench, in that it was smoother but also extremely clear. It occurred to the Elder that the cornstalk's dry spots probably already covered the entirety of each leaf, and might even have spread to the plant's stem. He reflected, *As long as the dry spots don't reach the center of the stalk and the top remains green, the plant can still be saved.* As the Elder was thinking this, he again heard the lead wolf's piercing howl. His body began to tremble, and he vigorously blinked his eyes. He said to himself, *Apart from this pack of wolves, you mustn't think about anything else. If you keep getting distracted, you will surely die.* Fortunately, the wolves hadn't noticed that the Elder's attention had strayed. As the wolves were about to advance following the lead wolf's howl, the Elder waved his carrying pole. The pole struck the sides of the gully, and as the cold sound wafted over, the wolves began to retreat.

A deadlock hung over the Elder and the wolves like a suspension bridge, and each time they blinked it would sway back and forth in a terrifying manner. The Elder could not see where exactly the wolves' bodies were, so instead he stared at the wolves' green eyes, and each time the eyes moved, he would swing his pole and force them to retreat. Time was like a silent ox pulling a cart, slowly crushing the Elder's will. The moon emerged, and was as round as the wolves' eyes. The Elder felt as though an earthworm were crawling down his back. He knew that his back was covered in sweat, and felt the aching in his legs penetrate his body like daggers. His energy was sapped more by the current deadlock than by his previous exertions. He hoped that the wolves would grow tired of standing there and instead would lie down, or at least move around a bit. Instead, they continued standing motionless in a semicircle five or six paces from the Elder, staring at him intently, like weathered rocks. The Elder could even hear the soft creaking sound of their eyes shifting back and forth, and could see that the fur on their backs had a tint of fire as it rustled in the breeze. The Elder wondered, *Can I outlast them?* He told himself, *You must outlast them, even if it kills you!* The Elder thought, *Each of them has four legs, but you only have two, and furthermore are an old man in your seventies.* The Elder said, *My God, night has only just fallen, yet your body is already so cramped up. Surely you don't want to deliver yourself into the wolves' jaws!* One of the cubs couldn't stand still any longer, and when the lead wolf wasn't looking, it lay down, after which the other cub lay down as well. The lead wolf looked at the two cubs, and emitted a purplish-red roar. The cubs bowed their heads and made yelps like blades of green grass. Then, the pack fell silent. The weariness began with the cubs, but after they lay down the Elder seemed to become infected by their exhaustion, and his own legs turned to rubber. He wanted to move, but in the end he merely tensed his tendons and shifted his knee caps, then stood straight again. He couldn't afford to let the older wolves see that he could barely remain upright. He thought, *If you reveal just a bit of exhaustion, they will immediately attack. If you can manage to stand here without moving a muscle, you may live, but if you start to sway, you'll surely die.* The moon, partially occluded by clouds, moved across the sky from east to west. He smelled the clouds' parched scent, and realized that the next day there would again be clear skies. If he were to weigh the sunlight on the mountain top, it would weigh at least five or six *qian*. The Elder glanced up, and saw that there was a dense cloud in front of the moon, and he thought, *Once the moon reaches the cloud, the cloud's shadow will pass over the gully.* Like a sturdy tree, he waited until the shadow passed overhead, and as soon as it covered him like a silk sheet, he took the opportunity to quietly stretch both legs in succession. He instantly felt the *qi* passages in his legs and his upper body connect, as a burst of vital energy surged to his knees. He straightened his body, and the carrying pole hooks produced a sound like that of wet paper ripping. At that instant, the same shadow passed over the wolf pack, and the Elder saw the mass of green eyes move toward him like a swarm of fireflies. He roared, and furiously swung the carrying pole hooks against the sides of the cliff. Rocks and sand fell to the ground beside his feet, like water cascading down. He waited for the sound to subside, as clouds drifted past the opening of the gully. He saw that five of the wolves were now standing only four or five paces from him. Fortunately, he had been able to stretch as the cloud's shadow was passing overhead, and consequently he was now able to make a loud movement, halting the wolves' advance and permitting the stalemate to continue deep into the night.

He thought, *I'm already seventy-two years old, and have endured countless more hardships than you.*

He thought, *As long as I'm in the opening of this gully, surely they won't dare come any nearer.*

He thought, *How can wolves be afraid of a man standing here motionless?*

He said to himself, *You absolutely mustn't doze off—because if you do, you're doomed. Blindy and the cornstalk are both depending on you.*

The two cubs lying on the ground both had their eyes closed. The Elder saw that the brightest two pairs of green eyes were extinguished like lanterns. He discretely moved his right hand forward on the pole, and when his right hand reached his left, he pinched his left wrist. He felt the pain surge from his wrist to his eyelids, and his fatigue shuddered as though it had just been seared by a flame. The fatigue dripped from his eyelids into the moonlit gully, and only then did he move his hand back. Another wolf lay down, and its eyelids immediately covered that bright green light. The lead wolf snorted, and the other wolf opened its eyes again.

In the middle of the night, the time began to sound green and luxuriant. Overhead, several stars seemed to be missing and the moonlight had a kind of tragic coolness. The Elder blinked several more times. He discretely raised one foot and used it to step on his other one, and only then did he feel his eyelids begin to soften. Looking at that moon and stars above, he felt he had managed to make it through more than half the night. The second half was already approaching, like a distant bell tolling the hours. At this point, as long as he could manage to keep standing there without a sound, his drowsiness might be transmitted to the wolves themselves.

Like dampness, this drowsiness did in fact begin to overcome both the Elder and the wolves. Three more wolves lay down. The lead wolf snorted again, but couldn't stop the others, until eventually the lead wolf was the only one left standing. Upon seeing that the original array of green eyes had been reduced to only two, the Elder felt somewhat relieved, and thought to himself, *If only the lead wolf would lie down as well. As soon as it does, I'll be able to quietly stretch my arms and legs.* But not only did the final wolf not lie down, it instead came up to the front of the pack. Thinking that the wolf was trying to cut off his only means of retreat, the Elder suddenly found his back covered in cold sweat. He furiously swung his pole, but between swings the wolf came to a halt, stared, then walked in a semicircle in front of him, before finally withdrawing to where the other wolves were lying on the ground. Then, the lead wolf lay down and closed its eyes as well.

All of the green lanterns were now extinguished.

The Elder sighed. His legs felt weak, but just as he was about to collapse his heart began to pound and he stood up straight again. At that instant, he noticed that the lead wolf was peeking through its half-closed eyes, then closed them again. The Elder didn't sleep, convinced that the lead wolf was simply waiting for him to doze off. He picked up a long vine, removed his belt, and unfastened the carrying pole's two cords. Then he tied them all together to form a long rope. As he was doing this, the Elder deliberately made a loud racket. He noticed that four wolf eyes were watching him, then they closed again.

This time the wolves had really fallen asleep.

Under the soft white moonlight, the nine sleeping wolves resembled a field of freshly turned earth, and a stench emanated from this uneven ground. The Elder removed his shoes and, holding his breath, tiptoed forward a couple of steps. He tied one end of the rope across the opening of the gully, then took a couple of steps back and tied the other end around his own wrist. Finally, he leaned the carrying pole against the sides of the gully, and closed his eyes.

The Elder went to sleep.

The Elder slept as sweetly as fragrant grass, and time swept through his dreams like a whirlwind. Whenever the Elder felt a tug on his wrist, his dreams would be violently interrupted. He would open his eyes, pick up the carrying pole, and point it at the wolves.

The sky finally began to brighten, and the moon and stars quietly disappeared from sight. In the entrance to the gully there was a layer of dark blue. The Elder blinked, and saw that the wolves had broken the portion of the makeshift rope that he had placed several paces in front of him, though the belt portion of the rope was still blocking their escape. The wolves knew that the sound had woken the Elder, so they stood there uneasily, carefully watching both the Elder and his snakelike red belt. As the Elder gripped the carrying pole, he felt a shooting pain, then pointed one end of the pole at the center of the wolf pack. He saw that there were still five wolves in front, but didn't know where the other four had gone. The lead wolf was no longer in front of him either. The Elder blanched but continued staring straight ahead, though his heart was pounding loud enough to knock down houses and buildings. He knew that if even one of those four missing wolves managed to sneak up behind him, this night's deadlock would be shattered and he would die.

The Elder listened intently.

The cold sweat soaked the bottoms of his shoes, and he felt as though he were standing in two pools of cold water. The Elder struggled to determine where the lead wolf could have led those other three midsize wolves. He looked around the opening of the gully and saw a sheen of golden sunlight. He realized that the sun had finally come out. Wolves are nocturnal creatures that cannot tolerate sunlight, and if on that day the sun was as blindingly hot as it had been, these wolves would surely retreat before it reached its full strength. As the Elder was thinking this, he noticed the smell of urine. He was about to see which wolf was the source, when he was distracted by clumps of earth falling on his head from the cliff above.

The Elder and the wolves simultaneously looked up at the top of the cliff, where the Elder saw that the lead wolf was leading a cub toward the entrance of the gully. The Elder then glanced over at the other side of the gully, where he saw another pair of half-grown wolves heading down toward the base of the hill. The old man suddenly realized that while he was sleeping, those four wolves had separated from the main group and proceeded to the top of the cliff, to find a way down to the gully behind him. Unfortunately for the wolves, the gully was too narrow and the cliffs were as steep as walls, and in the end they had no choice but to return in the direction from which they had come. The Elder felt secretly pleased, and his body began to radiate strength like the sun. At this point, the sunlight began to stream into the gully, and up on the cliff the lead wolf howled in frustration. When the five wolves standing in front of the Elder heard this howl, they looked up and examined the Elder and his pole, then turned and headed back toward the entrance of the gully.

The pack retreated.

After maintaining the deadlock for an entire night, the wolf pack finally retreated. As the wolves walked away, they periodically glanced back at the Elder. The Elder was still holding his pole as he watched the wolves retreat. When they reached the entrance, they all turned and stared at him for a moment, then left the gully. Their footsteps gradually faded away, until the sound died out altogether, like autumn leaves falling to the ground. The Elder released his grip and finally dropped the carrying pole. He suddenly felt as though there were bugs crawling up his legs. He looked down, and realized that the urine he had smelled had not been from the wolves, but rather had been his own.

He had been so terrified that he had wet himself without realizing it.

The Elder slapped and cursed the object dangling between his legs, then sat and rested for a while. Seeing that the sunlight was growing brighter, he got up and grabbed the carrying pole, then headed toward the opening of the gully. He found an elevated area, then looked around to confirm that the wolves had, in fact, left. Only then did he place the carrying pole on his shoulders again and walk out with the two buckets.

After the Elder emerged from the gully, he went toward the mountain ridge to the west. Afraid that the wolves would return and realizing he still had a long way to go, he only rested for a moment before proceeding up the path to the mountains. The undulating path was still reddish brown, and in the sunlight it resembled the backs of a herd of cattle. The Elder placed the buckets of water on the ground and took a breath, then watched the wolves climb a hill in the distance, heading toward the Balou Mountains.

The Elder said, *Damn, did they want to fight me? Do they even know who I am? I am the Elder! I don't care if they are nine wolves—even if they were nine jackals, what would they be able to do to me?*

The Elder gazed in the direction where the wolves had disappeared, and shouted, *Don't fucking leave! Stay here with me for another day or two.* Then he lowered his voice and added, *Yes, go ahead and leave. This spring is mine—it belongs to me, Blindy, and the cornstalk.* The Elder remembered the stalk and its dry spots, and shuddered. He leaned over one of the buckets and drank until his belly was swollen with water, and he no longer felt thirsty or hungry. Then he picked up the buckets and proceeded along the mountain road.

By the time he got back to his field, it was already noon. After having spent an entire day and night looking for water and caught in the standoff with the wolves, the Elder felt as though he was now over a hundred. His beard had been thin and sparse, but overnight it seemed to have grown much longer. By the time he reached Baliban Hill, he was about to topple over like a rootless tree. As he was resting by the side of the road, the blind dog came to him. He noticed that the dog's tongue was cracked, yet its eye sockets were filled with pools of dark water. The dog wept. It had heard the old man's weak footsteps, had smelled the scent of fresh water, and then had staggered up the ridge toward him. When the dog was a few paces away from the Elder, however, it suddenly collapsed.

You need to come here, the Elder said to the dog. *I'm too tired to move.*

The dog crawled forward a couple of paces, then became as still as death. Only its eye sockets continued to well up with tears.

I know you're hungry and thirsty, the Elder said. *It's hard enough just to survive.*

Without a sound, the dog faced the Elder.

The Elder shuddered, and he asked whether the cornstalk had died. The blind dog lowered its head, its tears dripping to the ground.

Leaving the buckets at the top of the ridge, the Elder headed toward the stalk. He kicked up a cloud of dust as he staggered along, and when he reached the shed, his heart began pounding loudly. Under the sun's searing rays, the stalk's leaves didn't have a trace of green left. Even the ribs of the leaves, which had previously been light green, were now dark brown. *That does it*, the Elder thought, regretting that he had not been able to bring the water in time to save the stalk. *It was not you who defeated that pack of wolves, but rather it is they who defeated you. They must have known that the cornstalk had died, which is why they finally decided to leave. It turns out that they were not trying to devour you, but rather they held you up for an entire night precisely in order to ensure the death of this stalk.* Just as he was about to collapse, he looked at the tip of the stalk and saw that in the center of a circle of dry leaves there was a drop of green that struck his gaze with a thump.

The stalk was still alive, and even under the blazing sun it retained a trace of green. The Elder turned over one of the leaves, and saw that on the back there was a thin silklike layer of green, and a starlike array of green dots were visible in the areas between the dry spots. The leaf's ribs were like a bent bow, and there was a trace of steam slowly emanating from it.

The Elder returned to the top of the ridge, where he grabbed a bowl and used it to ladle out some water. Then he placed the water in front of the blind dog's mouth, and said, *The cornstalk is still alive, so leave me this bowl after you finish.* Then the Elder carried a bucket of water to the stalk. He leaned over the bucket and took a mouthful of water, pulled open the top of the cornstalk, then spit out the water. Immediately, a green bead appeared under the searing sun, and as the droplets the Elder spit out landed on the red-hot sunlit area, they produced a sizzling sound. The sunlight devoured the drops before they fell to the ground. The Elder spat seven mouthfuls of water onto the tip of the cornstalk, washing it as clean as though it had rained continuously for seven days and seven nights. After some of the green areas began to regain their original color, the Elder placed the bucket beneath the stalk, and used the bowl to ladle out water and carefully washed each of the leaves. As he did so, he used the bowl to catch the excess water, then poured it back into the bucket. The sound of dripping echoed through the thick sunrays. He washed one leaf after another, and by the time he was on the fourth leaf he saw the blind dog returning from the ridge with a bowl in its mouth. The dog placed the bowl by the shed, then walked over and stood next to the Elder's leg. The Elder asked, *Are you thirsty? There is a spring and plenty of water for you to drink.* The blind dog shook its head, then ran its paws over the surface of the leaves.

The Elder said, *These leaves are still alive. You can relax.*

Standing next to the Elder's legs, the blind dog let out a long sigh, then lay down. It had a gentle and relaxed expression.

As the Elder was going to fetch more water from the pond, he noticed that behind the blind dog there was a black mass resembling a rotten eggplant. When he went to look closely, he saw that the black mass had a reddish tint, and when he tried to kick it, he discovered that it was actually a dead rat. He turned around and saw that there were several more rats inside the enclosure, and when he went back outside he discovered that there were seven or eight more rats lying around, and each of them had red splotches and what looked like bite marks. Obviously, the blind dog had killed them. The Elder called over the blind dog and asked it whether or not this was true. The dog took the Elder's hand in its mouth and pulled him over to the roots of the cornstalk. The Elder saw that rats had gnawed on the stalk's roots, and sap was seeping out. Illuminated by the sun's rays, the sap resembled a bluish-yellow blob. The Elder sat down in front of the stalk's wound and caressed the ball of dried sap, then he patted the dog's head, and said, *Blindy, I'm very grateful to you. In the next life, if I become reincarnated as an animal, I want to become reincarnated as you. And if you become reincarnated as a human, I'd like for you to be reincarnated as my child, and live peacefully your entire life.* At this point, the blind dog's eye sockets filled with tears again. The Elder wiped away the tears, then brought another bowl of water and placed it in front of the dog's mouth, saying, *Go ahead and drink as much as you want. When I go fetch more water, you'll need to stand guard beside the cornstalk.*

The cornstalk was finally revived. For three days in a row, the Elder used buckets of water to irrigate the stalk, and on the morning of the fourth day, he saw that the tip of the stalk was green again. The green color from the back of every leaf had seeped through to the front, and was rapidly expanding like a drop of water on a sheet of straw paper. As the green areas expanded, the dry spots shrank. After several more days, when the Elder gazed at the stalk from the road, he could once again see the green leaves swaying back and forth in the sunlight.

The Elder and the blind dog proceeded to eat the remaining food, but eventually even the days when they could have half a bowl of broth came to an end. The first day that they

didn't have anything to eat, the Elder still hauled two buckets half-full of water back from the spring. When he went to
fetch more the next day, his sight grew blurry and he began to
stumble as soon as he reached the ridge. The Elder knew he
couldn't fetch any more water, so he returned from the ridge
and drank until his belly was full. On the third day, the old
man was leaning against one of the shed posts watching the sun
rise, and he saw that the moon had not yet set, even as the sun's
piercing rays were shining down on the ground. He hugged
the blind dog, and said, *Go to sleep, Blindy. After you fall asleep,
you can sate your hunger in your dreams.* The dog, however,
was unable to fall asleep. The sun was shining brightly on the
Elder's face and began to produce a burning smell, whereupon
he drank another half a bowl of water to sate his hunger, and
then he developed an urge to relieve himself. After peeing, he
became even more famished than before, so he drank several
more times, until there was only a single bowl of water left in
the bucket.

The Elder said, *I can't drink anymore. That last bowl is for
the cornstalk.*

The sunlight bore down on his head, and the sun's rays
now weighed five *qian*.

The Elder said, *Fuck your ancestors, you blasted sunlight.*

The sun's rays now weighed five and a half *qian*, as the
sun continued to bear down on his head.

The Elder said, *Can we continue to endure it, Blindy?*

The sun's rays now weighed almost six *qian*. The Elder
went to rub the blind dog's belly, which was as soft as a mound
of mud.

The Elder said, *You're even skinnier than I am. I've truly failed you, Blindy!*

He touched his own belly, and found that the skin was as thin as a sheet of paper.

The Elder said, *Blindy, you must sleep for a while. After you wake up, there will be something to eat.*

Without saying a word, the dog lay down at the old man's feet. Every hair on its body was long and thin, like sticks and twigs, and the tips of every strand were frayed. The Elder wanted to sleep, but every time he closed his eyes he would hear a rumbling in his belly. He endured this acute hunger for another day, and when the sun once again approached the western mountains, he finally fell asleep. When he reopened his eyes, he had a bright smile on his face. Leaning on one of the shed posts, he stood up and gazed at the setting sun. After estimating that the sun's rays now weighed less than four *qian*, he asked the sun, *Do you think you can outlast me? Who am I? I'm your Elder, that's who!*

The Elder peed a drop of urine in the direction of the setting sun, then said to the dog lying at his feet, *Get up. I told you when you woke up there would be food to eat.*

The blind dog struggled to stand. Its fur was disheveled and matted, and it gave off a brown, burning odor.

The Elder said, *Can you guess what we're going to eat?*

The blind dog faced the old man, a look of disappointment on its face.

The Elder said, *I'll tell you. We're going to have some meat.*

The dog continued to face the old man, staring blankly at him with its blind eyes.

The Elder said, *Really, we are going to have some meat.*

After the Elder said this, the sun cackled with laughter, then sunk below the mountains. In the blink of an eye, the searing heat dissipated, and a cool silklike breeze began blowing over the ridge. The Elder fetched a spade from beside the stove, then went to dig a hole at the end of the field. He dug a large, round pit, as though he were going to plant a tree. The pit was one and a half feet deep, and the edges were as smooth as a cliff. Then he lit a fire and boiled some water. He picked a tassel from the cornstalk, mixed it with the water, and ladled it out, pouring it into the pit. By this point, it was almost dusk, and the mountain ridge was so quiet you could even hear the footsteps of the approaching night. There was damp coolness emanating from the bottom of the gully, and it surrounded the old man and the dog like mist. They sat down in the shed and listened for any movement in the pit, waiting for the night's inky darkness to cover the field.

The Elder asked, *Do you think the rats will fall into the pit?*

The blind dog pressed its ear to the ground and listened carefully.

The moon shone onto the ground, and the ground along the mountain ridge was bathed in watery moonlight. In the silence, the blind dog did indeed hear the rats kicking the moonlight. The Elder quietly felt his way toward the pit, and found that inside there were three rats fighting for food. He quickly covered the pit with a sheet, as the rats stared up in astonishment.

That night, the Elder and the dog caught thirteen rats, and in the light of the moon they skinned, cooked, and ate them, as a fragrant stench wafted in all directions. They went to sleep just before daybreak, and woke when the sun was three rod-lengths high in the sky. The Elder tossed the rat pelts into the gully, then hauled the bucket to the pool forty *li* away.

From that day on, there was a period during which the Elder and the blind dog enjoyed a peaceful and uneventful existence. They dug several bottle-shaped pits—each with a narrow opening, a wide base, and smooth walls, such that after the rats fell in they wouldn't be able to crawl back out again. Every night, the Elder and the blind dog would bring back a dozen or so corn seeds from the fields, which they would grind and boil until a golden fragrance wafted in all directions. Then, they would pour the broth into the pits and retire to the cool shed to sleep. Sure enough, the next day there would be several rats—sometimes even a dozen or more—trapped in the hole and crying in terror, which would provide the Elder and the blind dog with enough sustenance for another day or two. Every other day the Elder would go to the pool to fetch more water, and in this way their schedule became as smooth as a river without any waves or ripples. About half a month after the crisis, the cornstalk, still alive within the enclosure, produced a thumb-sized bud of an ear. Finally able to relax, the Elder would sit in front of the ear and speak to the blind dog. Once he said, *Blindy, do you think tomorrow this ear will become as large as a rolling pin?* Seeing that the Elder was happy, the blind dog licked his leg. The Elder patted the dog's back, and remarked that normally a cornstalk needed a month and ten days from the time the ear first appeared until it was ready for harvest, so how could this one possibly mature overnight? Another time he said, *Look, isn't this ear already as thick as a finger?* The blind dog went to look at the ear, and the Elder said, *You're blind. How can you see? This ear is already thicker than my thumb.*

One day, the Elder returned with water, and after irrigating the cornstalk he proceeded to hoe part of the field, whereupon he noticed that the ear had already started producing milky-white silk that resembled an infant's fuzzy hair. The Elder stood in front of the ear and stared in amazement, then laughed and said, *It's almost ready for harvest. Blindy, do you see that? It's almost ready for harvest!*

Hearing no response, the Elder turned and saw that the blind dog was next to the gully eating the previous day's leftover rat pelts. There was a horrendous stench, and the ground was covered in rat fur. The Elder exclaimed, *Blindy, isn't that filthy?* The blind dog didn't respond, and instead headed toward the pit. The Elder followed the dog to the edge of the pit, and his heart began pounding as he saw that this time there was only a single rat inside. This was his smallest yield since he began trapping rats half a month earlier. The previous day there had been four rats, and the day before that there had been five. But now there was only one. The Elder proceeded to dig several more pits along other ridges, and in each he placed several corn tassels, but the following day half of the pits were still empty and the remainder had only one or two rats each.

Never again did the Elder enjoy the good fortune of having a dozen or more rats fall into a single pit, and consequently the days of abundant food and water had come to an end. The Elder went up the mountain ridge and, after using the scale to weigh the sunlight, he stood there facing the sharp light, as a feeling of terror welled up inside him. This feeling started as a single bud but quickly grew into a vast forest covering the entire mountainside.

The Elder collected a rat from one of the pits and took it back to skin and cook, then wrapped it in cloth. Next, he patted the blind dog's head and told it to guard the field while he was away. The Elder departed, and after walking aimlessly for a while, he passed five villages and finally reached the tallest peak in the area. He stopped and faced the sun, then took out his scale and weighed the sunlight. He sighed, sat down, and rested in the shade at the base of a cliff. The cliff was as steep as a wall, and clumps of dirt periodically fell from the top. The Elder saw that the fields in front of him were so dry and cracked that they looked as though a net had been thrown over them. He peered farther into the distance, and saw that the serpentine mountain ridge resembled an endless series of bonfires. After staring for a while, his eyes began to ache from the heat. He took a cloth bundle from his pocket, unwrapped it, and removed the dead rat. When he had initially cooked the rat, the meat had been bright red, but after only half a day it had turned as black as sludge. The Elder sniffed it, but found that its original fragrance had disappeared and all that remained was a foul gray odor and a faint moldy smell. However, after having spent all day walking through the mountains, he was absolutely famished. He tore off one of the rat's legs and was about to eat it, when he noticed that there were several tiny white objects moving around in the meat. He shuddered and was about to throw the meat away, but changed his mind.

The Elder closed his eyes, opened his mouth, and stuffed the rat inside. He bit off two-thirds of it, chewed vigorously, and swallowed the entire thing in two bites.

When the Elder opened his eyes, he saw that on the ground in front of him there were a couple of maggots, which instantly dried up.

As dusk fell, the Elder returned to his field and proceeded to sit beside the cornstalk all night without sleeping. Regardless of how much the blind dog tried to cozy up to him, the Elder remained unresponsive. He gazed at the sky, then looked at the corn ear that was in the process of turning red. Finally, after the sun rose, the Elder suddenly got up and headed back to the village.

The mountains appeared vast and silent. The blind dog followed the Elder for a few steps, then went back to stand guard by the cornstalk.

The dog waited for the Elder to return.

At midday, the Elder returned. He had rolled a large brown barrel back from the village, and positioned it next to the cornstalk. Then he went up the ridge to catch a large rat. Holding the rat by the neck, he took it to the shed and killed it with a cleaver, collecting the blood in a bowl. He fed the pelt to the blind dog, while he stewed the blood and cooked the meat. He drank the stewed blood, then wrapped up the meat, collected his buckets, and headed out.

The Elder wanted to bring back enough water to fill up the entire barrel.

The Elder calculated that there were a total of nine rats left in the thirty pits he had dug. Given that he and the blind dog would need to eat at least one rat a day to avoid starvation, that meant they would run out of food in nine days. Of all the corn seeds the villagers had planted a few months earlier, there was nothing left. The harvest season was approaching and the sunlight was becoming progressively heavier, and this was precisely when the cornstalk most needed water and nutrients. The Elder decided he had to fill the barrel within the next nine days, so that even if he and the blind dog died, the cornstalk would still have sufficient water and nutrients to produce an ear of corn. The Elder walked over from the mountain road, as one bundle of sunlight after another beat down on his body. He again smelled the stench of burning fur, so he put the rat in the bucket and covered it with his straw hat. He wiped the sweat pouring down his forehead with his finger, then licked it. He felt sweat dripping onto his knee, so he squatted down and sucked that, too. He did everything he could to prevent his sweat from evaporating in the sunlight. The good thing was that every morning before dawn he would take his buckets and proceed north, and by the time the sun came up and sweat started pouring from his body, he would be within five or six *li* of the pool, and therefore it would only be during these final five or six *li* that he would have to resort to drinking his own sweat. By the time the sun was directly overhead, he would have reached the pool, where he would drink until his belly was full, eat the rat meat, then carry a couple of buckets of water up the hill. On the way back, when he was thirsty, he would drink directly out of one of the buckets. At this point, the sunlight would weigh eight or nine *qian*. He would periodically hear the sound of his sweat pouring down. He didn't hate the sunlight, nor did he resent the drought, but as his legs were trembling he would ask himself, *Am I old now? In the village, there have been men in their seventies who were still able to father a child, so why can't I manage to carry a couple of buckets of water?* His legs were trembling uncontrollably, so he had no alternative but to put down the buckets to rest for a while. He leaned over one of the buckets and drank until his belly was engorged. The Elder calculated that every time he went to fetch some water, he would have to stop and rest at least twenty or thirty times over the course of the forty-*li* trip. Furthermore, every time he stopped to rest, he would drink some water. As a result, he would drink, then sweat, then drink some more. But regardless of how often he stopped to rest and how much water he drank, by the time he got back to the field, the two buckets of water he had fetched from the pool would inevitably have been reduced to one.

After five days, the barrel was only one-third full, but the Elder had already consumed five rats. The remaining four would be his food for the next four days. In the sunlight, the stalk turned dark green, but after the tassel began to turn red, the stalk paused to rest. The new ear was as long and thick as a daikon, but the silk still refused to turn black, and the tassel also refused to have even a trace of yellow. With the tassel not turning yellow and the silk not turning black, it seemed as though the corn had a long way to go before it was ripe. At dusk, when the mountains appeared bathed in blood, the Elder would stroke the corn's green ear. Its softness would give him a chill, as he wondered when it would ever ripen. Based on the stalk's growth rate, it would need at least another twenty or thirty days. He calculated that it had already been at least four months since the other villagers departed. Corn normally needed about four and a half months to ripen, but the repeated delays in this stalk's ripening filled the Elder's forehead with furrows of anxiety. He led the blind dog out to the pits he had dug, but they didn't find a single rodent inside. Facing the mountain ridge, the Elder lay down on the side of the road. The ground beneath him was burning hot, and the heat passed through his back and circulated through his body. The blind dog lay down beside him—so emaciated that it didn't seem to have the energy to get up again. There was a rat squeaking from hunger, and when the faint sound made its way to them from the pit, it aroused a seismic hunger in the Elder and the blind dog.

The blind dog stared in the direction of the rat's cries.

The Elder gazed up at the sky, as silent as the ages.

Later, the Elder rolled over and began making a loud movement. The blind dog assumed the Elder was finally going to say something, and quickly turned in his direction. The Elder, however, merely stood up and walked away without saying a word. He felt the corn ear's firmness, mumbled something incoherent, and then, in the light of the moon, grabbed the buckets and headed north.

That night, the Elder brought back another load of water. This time he didn't drink a single drop, and instead returned with two full buckets. He poured one and a half buckets into the barrel. From the remaining half bucket, he used several bowls to irrigate the cornstalk, and poured another several bowls into a basin, so that the blind dog could drink from it whenever it was thirsty. Afterward, he cooked several rats, collected his buckets, and headed off again.

Over the next three days, the Elder brought back a full load of water every night and half a load of water every day—until the barrel was full.

The Elder decided that since he retained a bit of strength and there was still a rat in one of the pits, he would go down to the spring to fetch water one last time. This final load of water would be enough to last him and the blind dog for several more days. He wasn't holding out hope that it would rain, but he did hope that he and the blind dog could survive until the corn ripened, and would finally be able to break open this ear of corn. The ear appeared to have about thirty-five seeds in each row, and at least twenty-three rows. That meant that one ear would contain several hundred seeds. Four and a half months had passed, and the harvest season was inexorably drawing nearer. At midday the Elder could already smell the sticky yellow scent of the corn ripening, and by midnight this scent had become as pure as sesame oil.

That night, while the moon was overhead, the Elder set out to fetch the final load of water. By the time he returned, it was already afternoon of the following day. On the road, he stopped to rest forty-one times, and drank an entire bucket of water. He took the remaining bucket to the top of the mountain ridge, where he rested until dusk. He was convinced he didn't have the strength to carry this bucket down to the shed, so instead he decided to cook and eat the remaining rat. That was the largest of the original nine rats—it was one palm long, and its eyes were bright red. But when the Elder reached the pit where the rat had been trapped, he discovered it was full of dog paw prints, rat fur, and blood stains.

The Elder squatted next to that pit until the sky was dark.

When the moon appeared overhead, the Elder finally laughed and, like a sheet of slowly cracking ice, began to speak. He stood up and, gazing out at the smoky shadows moving under the moonlight, remarked, *It's fine for you to eat it, because now that you've done so I can tell you that eventually either you will eat me and then live with the cornstalk, or otherwise I'll eat you.* The Elder thought, *I can finally say this to Blindy. For days, I've been waiting for this opportunity.* The Elder returned to the ridge to fetch the buckets of water he had left there. Although his legs were weak, he was able to slowly proceed forward and collect the water, then carry it down to the shed.

The blind dog was lying under the shed, but it immediately got up when it heard the Elder's footsteps. It seemed to want to walk over to the Elder, but instead retreated a few paces and lay down in the opening to the enclosure. The moon was bright and appeared to be covered with hot gas. The Elder placed the buckets next to the barrel, and removed the mat on top to check the water level. He took off his shoes and shook out the dirt and sand; then, after staring at the whip hanging from one of the shed's support posts, he coughed and said softly, *Blindy, come here.*

This was the first time in days that the blind dog had heard the Elder's voice. The dog struggled to get up and hesitantly took a step forward, then stood still, facing in the direction where the Elder was sitting, its sparse fur making a shivering sound. The Elder looked off into the distance, then said, *Blindy, there's no need to be afraid. If you ate it, that's fine. That was going to be our last bite of food, and I don't mind if you took my portion.* Then the Elder added, *There's one more thing I need to tell you, Blindy. There isn't a single rat or corn seed left in this entire mountain range. Within three days, you and I will be so famished that we won't even have the energy to utter a word. At that point, if you want to survive, you'll need to consume me piece by piece. Then you must guard this cornstalk, so that when the other villagers return, you can lead them over and let them pick the ear of corn. Otherwise, if you appreciate what I have done to support you these past four or five months and want to help me stay alive, you must permit me to consume you, so that I may survive until the corn ripens.* The Elder added, *Blindy, you must decide. If you want to live, then tonight you must leave and hide somewhere. In a few days, I will starve to death.* Upon saying this, the Elder wiped his face, as two rows of tears wet his palm.

The blind dog stood there motionless, waiting for the Elder to finish speaking before taking a few steps toward him. When the dog reached the Elder's knees, it slowly bent its front legs while keeping its rear legs straight. It lifted its skinny head and stared silently at the Elder with eyes that resembled empty wells.

The Elder knew the dog was kneeling before him.

After kneeling down, the dog got back up and slowly walked toward the stove, where it used its mouth to open the pot and retrieve something from inside. Then it returned to the Elder.

The dog brought over the object it had taken out of the pot, and placed it at the Elder's feet. It was a skinned rat, which was soaking wet and appeared purple in the moonlight. The

Elder knew at a glance that this rat was still full of blood, unlike the ones the Elder had killed, which bled out when he disemboweled them. The Elder picked up the piece of purple meat and examined it, and found that it was riddled with bite marks. He sighed, and said to the dog, *Why didn't you eat the rat yourself? When I said you could have it, I meant it. There was no need to save it for me.* The Elder suddenly regretted that he had raised the possibility that one of them might have to die in order for the other to survive. He examined the meat in the moonlight, and remarked, *The abdomen is completely purple. The meat probably won't taste as good as it would have had the rat been killed with a knife.*

The blind dog lay down next to the Elder and rested its head on his leg.

The Elder cooked the rat meat the next day, and gave the blind dog half. He said, *Eat it. You need to survive for as long as you can.* The blind dog refused, so the Elder forced the animal's mouth open and stuffed in the rat's head and three of its legs. The Elder then took the remainder and stood in front of the cornstalk, chewing carefully. He knew that after he finished these final two bites, their food supply would truly be exhausted, and he would have no alternative but to starve to death. If he had to die, then so be it. He was seventy-two years old, which was considered elderly in this mountain region. Despite the drought, during which time all the remaining food was consumed, he not only managed to survive another half a year, he even managed to grow this cornstalk that was already three heads taller than he, with long and wide leaves, and an ear as large as a daikon. As the Elder stared intently at the ear's silk, he swallowed the rat meat in a few bites, then put his finger in his mouth and sucked on it noisily. At that moment, something began fluttering down onto his face like snow. The Elder looked up, his finger still in his mouth, and saw that the top of the cornstalk, which had previously been yellowish-white, had turned reddish-black overnight, and tiny chaff-like flakes were now flying everywhere. That is to say, the cornstalk was starting to pollinate and would soon begin producing seeds, meaning that harvest time had almost arrived. The Elder looked at the sky, and saw ray after ray of blindingly white sunshine bumping into one another. *It would be better if there were some wind,* the Elder thought. *At this time of year, it is better if there's some wind. If there were wind, the pollen would be distributed quickly and evenly, and the sprouts would grow evenly and sturdily.* The Elder removed his finger from his mouth and wiped it on his pants. Then, he began carefully pinching the corn ear. Through the thick peel, the Elder could feel that inside the soft ear there was a layer of firm objects. The Elder's heart skipped a beat, as though a door had suddenly slammed shut. His hand remained poised over the ear and he continued to stare into the sky, his mouth tightly closed. A moment later, after confirming that the kernels were firm, it was as if a door had reopened, and a surge of excitement coursed through his body. An excited expression fell across his face, and it appeared as though there were a river flowing beneath his dark, wrinkled skin. His hands began to itch uncontrollably. He blew on them, then walked out of the enclosure, took the hoe that was hanging from the pagoda tree, and began digging around the cornstalk. Dirt rained down, as fine as wheat or millet, and carried a golden scent of autumn harvest. He continued digging around the cornstalk until he reached the reed mats, by which point he was so exhausted that his gasps sounded like a severed rope. He dismantled the enclosure and tossed the mats under the tree. The blind dog followed him, not knowing what else to do. Without a word, the Elder dug past the enclosure's support posts, then turned and dug a perimeter around the barrel. He continued until he accidentally struck the barrel, producing a sharp, moist sound. The Elder stopped and stood there, a bright smile on his face. He said, *Blindy, it's harvest time. The cornstalk has finally produced seeds!*

The blind dog licked its lips.

The Elder lay on the ground and said to the heavens, *The moment I've been waiting for has finally arrived. It's finally harvest time!*

The blind dog licked the Elder's fingers.

While being licked by the blind dog's ticklish tongue, the Elder fell asleep.

After he awoke, the Elder went to see that ear of corn, and the look of excitement immediately vanished from his face. He discovered that the stalk's leaves were not as green as before, and instead a layer of yellow was now showing through. This yellow layer was visible not only on the stalk's lowermost leaves, but also in the leaves that had just sprouted from the top. The Elder had been farming for his entire life, and recognized that this was a sign that the stalk lacked fertilizer. This was the period when the stalk was ready to ripen, but only with sufficient nutrition would it be able to produce all of its seeds. The best fertilizer was human night soil. In the past, the Elder always fertilized his fields with night soil, and consequently his crops—including wheat, beans, and sorghum—had always been the best in the village. Indeed, he was, without a doubt, the best farmer in the entire region. Standing in front of his cornstalk, his lips had become as dry as the drought-stricken ground along the mountain ridge, but he didn't go over to drink water, nor did he ladle out any for the blind dog to drink. He didn't know where he should go to find some night soil. The village's outhouses were all so dry they were enveloped in clouds of dust, and any excrement that remained had become so desiccated that it had less value as fertilizer than firewood. The Elder and the blind dog had both gone several days without needing to relieve themselves, since their intestines had absorbed most of the rat meat and bone residue they had managed to eat. The Elder remembered the rat pelts he had eaten, and he went to look for more, but couldn't find a single one. He suspected that the blind dog must have eaten them while he was out fetching water. Panting heavily, he climbed up from the base of the hill. He originally wanted to ask the blind dog about this, but in the end he merely went to the pot that had had the rat and drank a bowl of oily broth. He didn't cover the pot when he was finished, and instead turned and said to the dog, *Whenever you are hungry or thirsty, you should go drink.* Then the Elder took his grain sack and went to the village to look for fertilizer.

When the Elder returned from the village with an empty bag, he was leaning on a bamboo stick, and every three steps he had to stop and rest. Exhausted, he dropped the empty bag to the ground, then went to see the blind dog, who was still lying under the shed. The water in the pot was still as he had left it, and the same eleven drops of oil were still floating on top. He asked the dog, *You didn't drink any?* The dog moved weakly, and the Elder used a spoon to drink half a bowl of water, including five of the eleven drops of oil. Then he said to the blind dog, *The remainder is for you.* He went back to the cornstalk, and when he looked at the leaves he saw that the thin layer of yellow appeared to have grown darker, and the green now appeared to be submerged beneath the yellow. The Elder thought, *Why didn't you prepare some fertilizer earlier? Aren't you the village's Elder? Fuck your ancestors—why didn't it occur to me that the cornstalk would need extra fertilizer when it started to produce seeds?!*

That night, the Elder slept under the cornstalk, and when he woke the next morning he noticed that the green color of several of the leaves had completely faded, and instead the leaves were now covered with a paperlike sheet of yellow.

The following night, the Elder once again slept under the cornstalk, and when he woke the next morning he discovered that not only were two of the leaves completely yellow, but the silk on the ear of corn had prematurely dried out. He pinched the ear, and found it to be as soft as mud. Like the bones in his body, the semihard objects inside the ear had also disappeared.

The third night, the Elder yet again went to the cornstalk, but this time he didn't sleep and instead used the hoe to dig a trench. The resulting trench was half a foot wide, three feet deep, and five feet long—just the right size for someone to lie down, and more than large enough for a dog.

This was a grave.

Given that the grave was positioned right next to the corn-stalk, several of the stalk's roots were exposed to it. Once the Elder finished digging, he lay down to rest, then went to the stove to see whether the remaining half-bowl of meat broth—with the six drops of oil—was still in the pot. He wanted to drink some, so he picked up the spoon but immediately put it down again, saying to himself, *This last half-bowl was for the blind dog, but now three days have passed.* He said to the dog, *Blindy, three days have passed. Why haven't you drunk it yet?*

The blind dog was in the shed. It had been lying there motionless for three days, as the cool night air poured over its body. The dog lifted its head and stared, with its blind eyes, in the direction of the Elder's voice. The dog didn't follow the Elder's instructions, and instead merely rested its head on its front legs. By this point, a hazy light had begun to appear in the sky, and the darkness covering the mountain ridge was being replaced with the light of day. The Elder leaned over the barrel and took several sips of water, then took out a pair of scissors and used them to punch a hole in the base of the barrel.

After the Elder punched the hole in the base of the barrel and water started flowing out, he took some dirt and caked it over the opening. Having nothing else to do, he hung his hoe on the tree branch and lay his shovel next to the grave. He placed a mat over the top of the barrel, then folded his quilt inside the shed, gathered up his bowl, chopsticks, and spoon, and placed them under the shed post. Finally, he went to the stalk and examined the light yellow color that was gradually spreading over the leaves. He pinched the ear, which resembled a water bag. He turned around as the sun burst out from between two mountain peaks in the east, making the mountains appear as though they were drenched in blood. The Elder stood between the cornstalk and the shed, and gazed at the mountain ridge. It was as if there were thousands upon thousands of cattle running in all directions. He was so exhausted he couldn't even see straight. He rubbed his eyes, glanced up at the sky, and saw an array of scalelike clouds with silver linings hopping around in front of the sun, like countless fish swimming around in a pond. The Elder thought to himself, *Today the sunlight must weigh at least 1.4* liang. He turned and glanced at the scale hanging from the shed post, then edged over to the blind dog. He lifted the dog and placed it in the grave, rubbing its body against the four sides of the grave. Then he removed the dog, and said, *Blindy, either you or I will die, and whichever of us survives must bury the other in this grave.* The Elder stroked the dog's back and wiped the tears from its eyes. He took a coin out of his pocket and placed it heads-up, then rubbed the dog's right paw over it. He said, *Fate will determine whether we live or die. I'll toss this coin, and if it lands heads-up, you must bury me in this grave so that my body may serve as fertilizer; and if it lands heads-down, then I must bury you.*

The dog's well-like eyes stared at the coin in the Elder's hand, as murky blackish-red tears welled up in its eye sockets and dripped down into the newly dug grave.

There's no need to cry, the Elder said. *If after my death I am reincarnated as an animal, I want to be reincarnated as you. And if you are to be reincarnated as a human, you may be reincarnated as my child. That way, we can continue living together.*

The dog's tears stopped flowing. It made an effort to stand up, but its forelegs collapsed and it lay back down inside the grave.

The Elder said, *Go drink the final half-bowl of broth in the pot.*

The blind dog bowed its head toward the Elder.

The Elder said, *I'm going to toss this coin. Whichever of us still has any energy left can bury the other in this grave.*

The blind dog faced the ground.

After brushing the dog's back three more times, the Elder stood up. The sun was marching over toward the mountain ridge, and if you listened carefully you could hear a fire burning brightly in the void. The Elder cursed, *Fuck your ancestors!* He glanced down at the coin one last time, then turned to the dog and said, *I'm going to toss it.* He proceeded to throw the coin into the air. The sun's rays were as dense as trees in a forest, and the coin bumped against one ray after another, producing a bright clinking sound. When the coin landed, it tumbled over and over, slicing those rays of sunlight into countless individual shards. The Elder watched the coin as it fell, as though staring at an enormous raindrop that had suddenly appeared before him. The blind dog stood up as well. It heard the reddish-yellow sound the coin was making as it tumbled through the air, like a ripe apricot falling onto the grass.

The Elder walked over to the coin.

The blind dog followed him.

The Elder reached a clump of earth he had dug up and, without bending over all the way, he stood up again. He sighed, and said calmly, *Blindy, go finish that final half-bowl of broth, which will grant you enough energy to bury me.*

The blind dog stood there without moving.

The Elder said, *Go on. Do what I say. After drinking the broth, you'll have to bury me.*

The dog still didn't leave. Instead, it bent its forelegs and once again bowed down to the Elder. The Elder said, *Blindy, there's no need to bow. It is Heaven's will that I should serve as fertilizer for this cornstalk.* Then, he picked up the coin, patted the dog's head, and said, *If you feel bad about this, I could flip the coin twice more, and if it lands heads-up two times out of three, then I die; and if it lands heads-down two times out of three, then you die.*

The blind dog stood up.

The Elder tossed the coin again, and it landed in front of the blind dog. The Elder took a look, and announced there was no need to toss it again. Then he sat down limply. The blind dog went over to where it had heard the coin fall. It touched the coin with its paw, licked the coin with its tongue, then lay down, as tears streamed down its face. Instantly, two pools of mud accumulated beneath its head.

Go drink that final half-bowl of broth, the Elder said. *Afterward, you can bury me.* Upon saying this, the Elder got up and went over to the shed post, where he pulled out a thin bamboo pole. The hollow pole was more than two feet long, and when you blew on it, it sounded very melodious. He inserted the pole horizontally into the hole he had punched in the base of the water barrel, then sealed the area around it so that no water would leak out. Next he pressed down on the other end of the pole, and a series of jade-like drops of water dripped out of the barrel onto the soil around the cornstalk. Immediately, the soil began to produce a greenish-red sucking sound, leaving behind a large wet area.

The Elder used some loose soil to erect a ring around the base of the cornstalk, to prevent the water from flowing away. After finishing this delicate task, he brushed the dirt from his hands, then looked up at the sun. He took out his scale to weigh the sun's rays, and found that they now weighed 1.5 *liang*. Then he took his whip, stood in an empty area, and whipped the sun more than a dozen times, until shards of light rained down around him like pear blossoms. Finally, exhausted, he hung up the whip, cleared his throat, and announced to the sun, *If I, your Elder, want to continue raising this cornstalk, what are you fucking going to do about it?*

From the sun's rays he heard a hoarse reply, like a broken gong. The sound progressed from this hill to the next one, going farther and farther until it finally disappeared. The Elder waited until the sound had completely faded away, whereupon he rolled up one of the mats and headed toward the grave he had just dug. Then he said to the blind dog, *After burying me, you should go north, following the road I told you about. When you reach the gully with the spring, you will find water, and the ground will be covered with bones left behind by the wolves. You can live there until the drought passes and the villagers return. But I won't be able to make it, given that I'll die either today, tomorrow, or the next day.* The sun was shining on the Elder's forehead, and the bits of dirt in his hair made a clanging sound as they bumped against one another. After the Elder finished speaking to the blind dog, he brushed the dirt from his hair and lay down in the grave, against the side where the roots of the cornstalk were. He covered his body with a mat, then said to the blind dog, *Bury me, Blindy. Bury me, then go north.*

The mountains were silent. The flames hidden in the searing sunlight suddenly became more energetic. In the boundless emptiness, a burning smell began spreading across the entire mountain ridge. The mountains and gullies, villages and roads, and dried-up riverbeds—they were all full of a thick and sticky sunlight that resembled a golden soup.

It was generally assumed that if it didn't rain in autumn, it would definitely snow the following winter. This year, however, winter came late, and it proved to be very dry. The drought continued unabated until the end of the following summer, at which point, rain clouds finally appeared. For half a month, the clouds repeatedly accumulated and dispersed, until finally it began to rain. A darkness then hung over the mountain range for forty-five days, as though the sun had been covered by a shroud. The rain blanketed the earth, flooding the entire land, and by the time the rain stopped and the skies cleared, it was already the autumn sowing season. Villagers gradually began to return to the ridge, bringing back their bedding, dishes, and children. At night, their halting footsteps resonated brightly under the moonlight. During the day, the mountain ridge once again became fully populated, with the jumbled sounds of people pulling carts, carrying loads, and talking; and over the mountain ridge, every now and then, there would be the sound of trees and vegetation coursing down like a river.

By this point, the autumn sowing season had arrived, but the villagers were shocked to discover that their autumn seeds were missing. In fact, there were no seeds at all in the entire several-hundred-square-*li* area of the Balou Mountains.

Suddenly, one of the villagers remembered how the Elder had stayed behind to look after a corn seedling. The villagers rushed out to the Elder's plot of land, and from a distance they could see that in the entire field there was only a solitary shed. When they reached the shed, they saw that the area the Elder had hoed was now full of grass that looked as though it had been planted, producing a thick layer of green that emanated the blue scent of fresh barley and a light white odor. Throughout the entire mountain range, they heard these smells clanking together, the way that on a quiet night one might hear the sound of a river flowing. In this green field, the villagers saw the cornstalk that had already matured the previous year. Its tip had been broken off and its stem was now as thick as a small tree. The stalk was next to two reed mats that were leaning over, and its leaves were covered in mold. Some of the leaves had fallen to the ground, while others were still growing. The stem, meanwhile, looked as though it were covered in paper that had been soaked in water and then dried out again. Hanging from the stalk there was an ear of corn as large as a wooden club used for washing clothes, and it was swaying in the wind. When the ear's jet-black tassels were touched, they would fall to the grass like wilted flower petals. The villagers picked this ear and quickly shucked it, and discovered that inside this enormous ear, which was as thick as a man's calf and as long as an arm, there were thirty-seven rows of corn. But out of those thirty-seven rows, there were only seven fingernail-sized grains that were as bright as pieces of jade, and all the rest had dried up before they had a chance to ripen.

These seven grains of corn were arrayed against a desiccated backdrop, like stars in a night sky. The villagers stared at this ear with only seven grains. They stood silently in the shed looking around, until finally they saw that the mat that had once been on top of the barrel had been blown over to the stove. Inside the barrel there wasn't a single drop of water, merely a thick layer of dirt. The thin bamboo pole that had been inserted into the base of the barrel was already cracked in multiple places. A bowl and spoon were still sitting on one side of the barrel, and a whip and scale were hanging from one of the shed's posts. About five feet from the barrel, on the grass right next to the cornstalk, there was a grassy mound. There was also a trench about half a foot wide, five feet long, and three feet deep. A dog was lying in the dense vegetation at one end of the trench, its scraggly body full of maggot holes. Its eye sockets were as empty as dark wells, and its entire body had been dried up by the sun. Gently, the villagers kicked the animal out of the trench as though it were a bundle of kindling, after which the grave-like shape of the trench became obvious. The villagers' hearts pounded, as they realized that this must be the Elder's grave. In order to move the Elder's body to the cemetery, the villagers dug up this pit. With the first shovel, they heard a bright clanking sound, as though they were digging up a metallic joint. They carefully removed the grass from the pit, and turned over the loose earth. Then every villager stared in shock, as they saw that the Elder's underpants had decomposed into soil. His entire body had disintegrated and every joint had come apart. There was a pungent white mist rising like smoke. The Elder was lying in the grave, with one arm in the process of reaching out to the cornstalk while the rest of his body huddled around the base. His corpse was riddled with maggot holes, which were much more numerous than the dog's. Each of the stalk's roots resembled a long and thin vine, and had a pinkish tint. The roots were growing into the Elder's body through the holes in his chest, thighs, wrists, and abdomen. There were several red roots as thick as chopsticks growing right through the Elder's decayed body and into his skull, ribs, and arm and leg bones. There were several reddish-white tendrils growing into his eye sockets and poking out through the back of his skull, gripping the packed earth along the bottom of the grave. Every joint and every piece of flesh had been transformed into a web of roots, tightly linking his body to the cornstalk itself. It was at this point that the villagers noticed that the cornstalk now had two stems, which had managed to survive the previous winter and summer and still retained a trace of green.

After some deliberation, the villagers reburied the Elder in his original location, and also buried the dog, which now resembled dried grass, in that grave right next to him. The smell of fresh earth was mixed with a thin layer of warm putrefaction. Finally, as the villagers were about to leave, someone noticed that in the shed, under the Elder's pillow, there was a rain-soaked calendar. In the grass outside, someone found a coin covered in rust. When they wiped away the rust, they noticed that the coin had text on both sides—meaning that both sides were "heads." No one had ever seen a coin with text on both sides before. The villagers passed it around, then tossed it into the air. The sun was shining brightly, and in the air the coin collided with one bundle of sunrays after another, producing a sound like red flower petals. The coin fell to the ground, then rolled into a ditch.

The villagers took the calendar back with them.

Eventually, it was harvest season again. After the villagers of the Balou Mountains had finished the food they brought back with them, they had been unable to find any corn seeds to sow, and many of them left in search for food. Within half a month, the entire region was completely depopulated, and in the process became so peaceful you could even hear the bright sound of the sunrays knocking against one another and the moonbeams striking the ground.

In the end, the only people left were seven men from seven of the village's households. They were all young and strong, and proceeded to build seven sheds on seven different mountain ridges. On seven nonadjacent plots of land, under the unremitting sunlight, they planted seven corn seedlings, each of which was as tender as oil.

MARROW

Chapter One

The entire world smelled of autumn.

The fall harvest season arrived before you knew it. In the mountains, the sweet smell of corn was so thick it would stick in your throat. Drop by drop, the autumn light streamed down onto the roofs of houses, onto the tips of grass, and onto the hair of the peasants out working in the fields. This sunlight, shimmering like agate, illuminated the entire village.

It illuminated the entire mountain ridge.

It illuminated the entire world.

It was a bountiful harvest. During this period of the year, a dry spell would usually be followed by a flood, and by the time the corn was ready for pollination, the balance of sun and rain would be perfect. Down in the plains the harvest was meager, while up in the mountains it was extraordinary. The ears of corn were almost as thick as a man's leg, leaving the stalks doubled over like a hunchback. A few of the stalks were broken and lying on the ground, struggling to grow. You Village, often called Four Idiots Village, consisted of a few hills, and had abundant harvests. Between the white dew and the autumn equinox—which is to say, between the fifteenth and the sixteenth solar terms—people began harvesting corn. All the land belonging to the family of Fourth Wife You was on the mountain ridge farthest from the village. During previous years' land reallocations, all of the families in the village felt that this field was too far away. The village chief told Fourth Wife You that if her idiot children wanted to eat, she would need to farm the field herself, and she was welcome to farm as much of it as she wished. Fourth Wife You therefore took her four children with her to sow the field. She sowed the entire ridge, amounting to perhaps eight or ten *mu* of land, but who knew this year would yield such an extraordinary harvest?

Fourth Wife You took her idiot children out to the fields three days in a row, and spent another three transporting everything back, but still had only harvested a third of her grain. By this point, she was exhausted, and found herself increasingly annoyed by this extraordinary harvest. In the endless cornfield, green stalks and dried leaves were piled high, and stepping inside was like entering the sea. As Fourth Wife You was carrying the baskets of corn up to the head of the field, she heard her Third Daughter calling softly out to her, "Ma, Ma! Won't you do something about Fourth Idiot? He keeps following me around, touching my breasts and pinching my nipples." By this point, there was already a huge pile of corn at the head of the field. The sky was high and the clouds were sparse. The purple strands of corn silk were just beginning to emerge, and they swayed back and forth in the sunlight. Fourth Wife You turned in the direction of the voice, and sure enough her son was chasing her daughter around. He had ripped open her dress, and her swollen breasts, white as a rabbit's head, were bouncing about as though they were about to hop out of her clothes. Fourth Wife You stared in disbelief. She saw no shame on her Third Daughter's face as Fourth Idiot grabbed her breasts. Instead, her face had a light glow, like a New Year's painting. Behind her, Fourth Idiot giggled, desiring his sister yet fearing his mother, his mouth full of saliva and his eyes full of tears. Fourth Wife You didn't know what exactly had led to this. Part of her wanted to get to the bottom of things, but at the same time she recognized that her children were idiots and she didn't know how to begin to ask them. As she stood there, something flashed before her and suddenly her husband, Stone You, appeared at the head of the field. He said that Fourth Idiot had grabbed the buttons on Third Daughter's dress, and that he had seen it all clearly from the field. Fourth Wife You shifted her gaze from her husband back to her son, and said, "Fourth Babe, come over here. Mother wants to tell you something." The boy came over hesitantly, and Fourth Wife You slapped his face.

Fourth Idiot grabbed his cheek and began sobbing.

Fourth Wife You roared, "Don't you know that Third Daughter is your own sister?"

Fourth Idiot headed into the cornfield like a dog with its tail between its legs. He sat on a pile of corn stalks, staring into the sky and bawling. Soon, the entire hillside was filled with his cries.

Thinking the storm had passed and that they needed to get back to harvesting the corn, Fourth Wife You emptied the basket on the ground and told her husband, "You can go do your thing, I'll continue working until nightfall. You don't need to keep returning." She turned around and saw Third Daughter staring at her intently, as if she were dying for something to eat.

She said, "I've already beaten your brother. What more do you want?"

Third Daughter said, "Ma, I want a husband. I dream of having a husband, like my two sisters, to hug when I sleep."

Fourth Wife You stared at her in shock.

Her husband also stared in shock.

Standing next to the pile of corn, Fourth Wife You looked at her daughter, who was a full head taller and half a body wider than she, whose breasts were as large as mountains. She suddenly realized that her daughter was already twenty-eight years old. By the time she herself was twenty-eight, Fourth Wife You had already given birth to four children, and it was also when she was twenty-eight—when Fourth Babe was six months old—that her husband decided to blow out his own flame. That day, she carried her son to the township clinic, and it was the clinic's doctor who blew out the final flame of the You family lamp.

Fourth Wife You was seventeen when, humming a line of opera, she married into the You family. She got pregnant a year later, and proceeded to have another child every eighteen months or so. After her first child, she lay on the postpartum bed and enjoyed having her husband wait on her, and hummed continuously for an entire month. What she didn't know was that her eldest, second, and third daughters would all turn out to be idiots. At the age of six months, their eyes grew dull and their pupils shrank. They didn't learn to speak until they were three or four, and at the age of five or six they were still playing with pig shit and horse urine on the ground. Even as teenagers, they were wetting their beds and soiling their pants. After seeing three children in a row turn out to be idiots, Fourth Wife You and her husband didn't dare have any more, and they didn't dare sing a single line of opera. But after several years of not having children, they decided they wanted a son and, full of hope, the couple set to work. In the end, Fourth Wife You gave birth to a son. By six months he could already speak, and by eight or nine months he could run around. Thinking that she had finally given birth to a bright one, she and Stone You would sometimes recite to their son several lines from a play. When the child was eighteen months old, however, he came down with a fever. This initially appeared to be an ordinary illness, but the fever continued overnight. When his parents examined him the next morning, they found that his mouth was crooked and his eyes were slanted. He could no longer speak, and couldn't even hold a rice bowl. He giggled and stared into space, and didn't seem to be aware of anything.

Everyone in the village was astonished by this development. Fourth Wife You and Stone You's faces and bodies—and their rooms and courtyard—all turned black and then white from the devastating news.

The villagers told them to go quickly to the clinic. So, they went.

The doctor asked, "How many brothers does the boy have?"

Fourth Wife You said, "He has three older sisters."

The doctor asked, "Are his sisters all right?"

Fourth Wife You replied, "Their minds . . . are not all there."

The doctor paused and looked intently at Fourth Wife You for what seemed like an eternity. He asked whether there was anyone else in her family who suffered from this illness. Fourth Wife You said no, there wasn't, and added that both of her parents were wholers. The doctor asked about her grandparents, and she said that they were wholers as well. The doctor asked about her great-grandparents, and Fourth Wife You replied that she had not met them but her father had told her that her great-grandfather could still do the lion dance at the age of eighty-two, and that her great-grandmother could still belt out opera at the age of seventy-nine. As the doctor continued his questions, he shifted his gaze to Stone You.

"How about you?" he asked.

Stone You fell silent.

Fourth Wife You tapped her husband on the shoulder and said, "He's asking you."

Only then did Stone You stammer, "My father had epilepsy, and when I was three years old he had an episode while plowing the ridge, and fell into a ravine and died."

Fourth Wife You's face hardened.

The doctor sighed and said, "You should return home. This illness can skip a generation, and there is no cure. You have four children and all four are idiots. You could have eight, and you'd have eight idiots. If you were to have a hundred children, they would all be idiots as well. You should go home and think hard about how you'll care for your four children for the rest of their lives."

The parents left without saying a word, and returned to their village in the depths of the Balou Mountains. On the way home, Stone You carried their son as he followed his wife. After leaving the clinic they exchanged a few words, but as the sun began to descend in the west, they stopped speaking. They were both exhausted, and the child on Stone You's shoulders drooled as he slept. As they approached the banks of Thirteen Li River just below the village, Stone You glanced at the flowing water, then back at the child on his shoulders. His son seemed to be grinning at him in his sleep. Suddenly, he began to tremble, and his eyes rolled back into his head. The sight startled Stone You, but the child's unnatural appearance quickly disappeared as he fell back asleep—half-crying and half-laughing.

Stone You continued standing next to the river, staring intently at his idiot son's face.

Stone You's wife—who by this point had already walked away—turned and shouted, "Come . . . quickly . . . otherwise the heat will be the death of us."

He said, "Why don't you carry our son over to the tree up ahead, to rest in the shade? I'll get a drink and then catch up with you."

Fourth Wife You took the child to a chinaberry tree and waited beneath it. She waited for what seemed like days, like months, like years, until dusk fell and the earth grew dark, but still there was no sign of her husband. She walked along the river, shouting, "Father of our child . . . father of our baby . . . where have you gone? Where have you gone, father of our child?" She walked several hundred steps and then, next to a pool, she saw Stone You, the father of her four idiot children. After he jumped into the river and drowned, his corpse had floated up to the riverbank like an old log. She sprinted down to the water's edge and dragged him to shore. She placed her hand under his nostrils to see if he was breathing and then, after a long pause, she sprinted down to the village to report his death.

Her man had killed himself, terrified of the future.

After her husband died, the light vanished from Fourth Wife You's life. When she was working in the fields there was no one to bring her shovels and sickles, and when she was resting there was no one to chat with. When the cistern froze over and cracked in the winter and she needed to bind it with wire, she had no choice but to do it herself.

During that year's harvest, Fourth Wife You tied her four idiot children to a tree at the head of the field as though they were dogs, then placed some grasshoppers, sparrows, stones, and tiles in front of them to play with while she was harvesting the wheat. She worked from dawn until noon, at which point she returned to the tree to rest—and discovered that her children had pelted the grasshoppers and sparrows with stones, pounding the sparrows on the tiles like crushed garlic until their heads were shattered and their blood was everywhere. The children were eating the sparrows' legs, wings, bodies, and heads, and their own mouths and faces were smeared red. Everything reeked of sparrow blood.

Fourth Wife You stared in horror. Eventually, she began sobbing—sobbing as though there was no tomorrow. Facing the mountain ridge where she had buried her husband, she cursed, "Stone You, you should have been tortured to death, but you've gone off to enjoy yourself, leaving me and our children to suffer in this world alone."

She added, "You call yourself a man? You've ruined me, and ruined our four children."

She continued, "Did you think that death would be the end of it? That you'd be able to rest in peace? I'm telling you, I won't let you rest until our children have their own families and their own jobs."

She continued, "Come back here! You've abandoned us in this world and gone off somewhere else."

She continued, "Come back here and kneel in front of me—kneel down and see your four children, then see how much wheat I harvested all by myself."

As Fourth Wife You cursed her husband, her voice grew weak and hoarse as her expression changed from one of fury to one of resignation. She dissolved into silence, but continued staring at an empty space in front of her. In an open space right between the wheat fields and the mountain ridge, there was an area that resembled a reed mat, full of rocks and weeds. Weeds grew out of the cracks between the stones, completely covering them with vegetation. Sure enough, her husband was kneeling in the clearing, crushing the wild grass beneath him. His gray shadow, thin as a cicada's wing, swayed between the green grass and the yellow stones. The other villagers who were out harvesting had already returned to the village to have lunch and sharpen their scythes, and then they would leave the village again, heading toward their own fields. Some of them were spreading the freshly harvested wheat to dry in the sun.

Her husband knelt there, at first looking up at her, and then down at the ground .

He said, "My entire life, I've never disappointed anyone as badly as I disappointed you."

He said, "I left you behind to endure pain and exhaustion."

He said, "Come what may, you must raise our children. When they have families and jobs, life will be easier for you."

As Stone You mentioned their children, Fourth Wife You looked behind her. Her four idiot children were still eating raw sparrows and grasshoppers, and her look of pain gradually faded and the color returned to her face. She picked up her scythe and began beating her husband like a madwoman, striking his head, his face, and his arms—whatever she could. The mountainside was filled with the sound of her blows, echoing from one side to the other. The sunlight was sliced into pieces by her blade, as was the long, cool breeze into burning hot segments.

The following year, she harvested the summer wheat but was unable to plant the autumn crops. Other families' autumn crops had already begun to sprout, but her own fields were bare. Each family's plow oxen worked endlessly day and night, and Fourth Wife You had no choice but to take advantage of the moonlight to hoe her field. She placed a mat on the ground, where her four idiot children could sleep, then took off her shirt and proceeded to hoe the field from one end to the other and back again. The freshly hoed soil had a moist and earthy smell that resembled dark crimson. The wheat sprouts gleamed in the moonlight, producing a warm and alluring white aroma. The red and white odors mixed together in the night air, like smoke and fog, and the sound of her hoeing and the sound of her snoring children trickled lazily through the watery moonlight. Fourth Wife You continued working until she was exhausted, but as soon as she sat down on the cool earth to rest, someone approached from the mountain ridge. It was a middle-aged man from a neighboring village, who came over and stuck his shovel in the ground at the head of the field. He looked at the topless Fourth Wife You and said, "Haven't you finished hoeing yet?"

Fourth Wife You quickly reached for her shirt.

The man laughed, and said, "No need to put it on. There's nothing I haven' t seen before." Fourth Wife You sat back down, her face and breasts both facing the man.

The man said, "Do you want some help?"

Fourth Wife You replied, "Sure."

The man asked, "What would I get in return?"

Fourth Wife You asked, "What do you want?"

The man said, "I'll hoe this entire field better than an ox could plow it, and break up the dirt as though I were milling grain. But you've got to sit there at the head of the field, so that whenever I turn around I can see your bare chest."

Fourth Wife You said, "Go ahead."

The man said, "When the field has been hoed, I'll plant your autumn crops. All I ask is that tonight you and I sleep together on that ridge."

Fourth Wife You said, "Don't waste time talking. Get to work."

The man leaned over and began hoeing. He did, in fact, hoe much better and much faster than she. He brought the hoe down vigorously and pulled it back and forth, then turned the earth over, the scent of fresh soil wafting over the field. At one point, the man looked up and stared at the topless Fourth Wife You, and asked, "You don't know how good your breasts look, do you?" He hoed some more, then looked up again and said, "I've been watching, and you've got the best breasts of anyone in the villages around here. Even after four children, they're still nice and firm." He hoed some more, then looked up again and said, "It's getting chilly. You can put your shirt back on, but don't button it." Fourth Wife You draped her shirt over her shoulders and covered her children with a sheet, then returned to where she had been sitting, with her breasts and chest facing the man.

He continued hoeing, walking backward along the field while periodically glancing over at Fourth Wife You's pert breasts. In order to see them more easily, he didn't hoe the field from one end to the other, but rather returned to the head of the field and hoed it again in the same direction as before. Every time he looked up, he said something sweet to Fourth Wife You. She didn't reply, and instead merely sat there with her breasts exposed and her arms either on her knees or resting at her side, permitting the man to watch her as he repeatedly approached and drew away. The mountain ridge was as quiet as a sleeping herd of cattle. Fourth Wife You's husband, Stone You, sat down behind her.

He said, "Don't you know who this man is? He is an ass from a neighboring village."

Fourth Wife You ignored him.

He said, "Mother of our children, I never imagined you could be so shameless. If the children woke up and saw you like this, and didn't open their idiot mouths to eat you right up, well, they would be no children of mine."

It was only then that Fourth Wife You turned and looked at him in the moonlight. With a "Pah!" she spat on the ground in front of him and said, "If you have any pride at all, go turn the earth yourself, like that ass."

Stone You said nothing more, and stood behind her, muttering. Fourth Wife You heard him begin to weep, but didn't say anything else and didn't look at him again. She just sat motionless, like a statue made of wood or clay, and remained there until only a narrow patch of land was left to be hoed, like a gray ribbon running along the edge of the ravine. By this point, the man was tired and had something else on his mind.

He said, "Let's sleep for a while. Then I'll finish."

Fourth Wife You replied, "Finish what you started, and the sleep will be all the sweeter."

The man said, "That triangular bit at the front, too?"

Fourth Wife You said, "That, too. I can grow forty or fifty stalks on it."

In the end, the white wheat stubble in the gully became invisible, and the ground appeared dark red under the now moonless, nearly starless night, as soft as if it were laid with a thick layer of crimson flowers. There was dew on the tips of the grass at the head of the field.

The eldest daughter sat up and, without opening her eyes, peed on the ground next to her youngest brother's feet, then lay back down. Her brother, finding his feet in a pool of steaming urine, pulled them away, rolled over, and murmured, "Ma, Ma! Who's boiling my feet in a pot?" Fourth Wife You went over to cover her children with the sheet, and said, "Go back to sleep. No one's boiling your feet."

At that point, the man walked over excitedly, treading on the soil he'd just hoed. He had broad shoulders and walked with vigor, each step making a small depression in the loose earth. Fourth Wife You watched him approach, and moved away from her children. In a flash, she had her arms in the sleeves of her shirt and was buttoning it up.

The man tossed his spade to one side, and asked, "Why are you buttoning your shirt?"

Fourth Wife You glanced at him.

"Do you plan to marry me? If you don't plan to marry me, then don't think of touching me."

The man stared in surprise.

"But we agreed—we agreed that if I hoed the entire field, we would spend the night together on this ridge."

Fourth Wife You said, "You also said you would help me plant the autumn crops. Have you done that?"

The man grabbed his spade angrily.

"I worked all night, and now it's almost dawn. If you won't sleep with me I'll split your head open with this spade."

Stone You turned pale and dropped to his knees before the man.

Fourth Wife You looked at Stone You, at the man's upraised spade, then at his furious expression. She calmly walked several steps toward the spade, squatted down beneath it, and said, "Then go right ahead and strike me down. I'm burdened with these four idiot children, and long ago lost my desire to live.

Strike me down and you won't even need to pay with your life. Just raise my four children for me."

The man turned to look at the reed mat on the ground, and saw that the four children had all woken up and were rubbing their eyes, staring at him and Fourth Wife You. He lowered his spade and planted his foot on Fourth Wife You's chest, saying, "Fuck, I might as well just rape you."

Fourth Wife You wiped the dirt from her chest and replied, "If you rape me, then I'll hang myself in your doorway. You still won't have to pay with your life, you'll just need to raise my four children until they all have families and jobs of their own."

The man stood there for a while, then walked away furiously.

The dawn came creaking in, interrupting the footsteps of the man in the distance, as well as the look Fourth Wife You exchanged with her husband.

And so Fourth Wife You got her field hoed, planted, fertilized, weeded, and harvested. Then, she moved on to the next season. One season followed another, just as night follows day—propelling her forward and propelling her children into adulthood. Her hair went gray, and she grew visibly older.

Chapter Two

In the middle of the harvest season, Third Daughter suddenly decided she wanted a husband and a family, and also to learn about sex. By the time Fourth Wife You was fifty, she had succeeded in finding husbands for her two elder daughters, and while they lived an impoverished life with their new families as they had with her, at least they had a life. Although both of her elder daughters were addled, when their illness wasn't acting up they could still sew buttons and count to ten. They knew how to go out and buy salt, and could bring back the correct change. They knew to bow their heads when a man looked at them, and only when their illness acted up did they fall to the ground, vomiting, foaming at the mouth, convulsing, and ultimately losing consciousness. But Third Daughter was different. She couldn't count to seven even when her illness wasn't acting up, and when she went to the village market to buy staples such as oil and salt, she never remembered to bring back the change. Whenever Third Daughter had her period, Fourth Wife You had to help her clean herself. Fourth Wife You had always assumed that Third Daughter would never have a chance to learn about sex, but now she was saying that she did in fact want a family and a husband, just like her elder sisters. Standing in the field of ripe corn, looking at her daughter's glow of excitement, Fourth Wife You saw some sparks in the sunlight fly between the cornstalks. The sky was high and the clouds were sparse, and the sound of corn being harvested on the ridge traveled toward them as clouds of dust rained down on the stems and leaves of the corn plants. The calm summoned Stone You from his grave, whereupon Fourth Wife You asked her daughter in his presence, "Daughter, what did you just say?"

Third Daughter straightened her neck and replied, "I want a family, and I want to be able to hug a man at night while I sleep, as my sisters do."

Fourth Wife You thought for a while, then asked, "What kind of man do you want?"

Third Daughter replied, "I want a wholer, not a cripple or a one-eyed freak. I want a good man, not the kind who would make me go into the fields to harvest corn."

Stone You said, "Daughter, don't you know what you are?"

Fourth Wife You said, "What is she? Whatever she is, she inherited it from your family."

Stone You said, "Can she find a wholer?"

Fourth Wife You spat on the ground and snorted. "We can look for a wholer, and if we can't find one, we can look for a semiwholer. You can go to each village on the mountain ridge and find a suitable man for our Third Daughter to marry."

At this point, Third Daughter looked at Fourth Wife You in surprise, and exclaimed, "Ma, you're crazy, too, and talk to people who don't even exist."

Fourth Wife You said, "Daughter, go pick some corn. If your brother tugs at your clothing again, you can slap him. After the fall harvest, and after we have planted the next crop, I'll find you a good family to marry into. I'll find you an even better husband than either of your two sisters have."

Third Daughter's eyes widened in surprise. Her mouth trembled and her cheeks turned bright red.

She hopped over into the depths of the cornfield. Immediately, the sound of harvest rippled across the ridge, like a river overflowing its banks. There was the smell of autumn and of cornstalks being trampled, which mixed together like smoke, blanketing the sky and the earth.

The mountain ridge was left completely bare after the hectic autumn harvest. The cornstalks had been cut down and left to dry at the head of each family's field so that they could be used as kindling in the winter. In the bare fields along the mountain ridge, some people had already begun plowing the earth and planting the next wheat crop, while others, because they had neither ox nor plow, had no choice but to take a shovel and do it by hand. Fourth Wife You led Third Daughter and Fourth Idiot to hoe the fields the first day. At one point, she went into a gully to pee, and when she returned she found that her daughter had unbuttoned her shirt and was giggling as her brother sucked her breasts.

Fourth Wife You simply stared. She knew she couldn't delay in finding Third Daughter a husband, so she picked up her spade and immediately took her children home, then proceeded to lock her son up in a room. Their house had a small garden, and the entire courtyard was filled with piles of corn and postharvest smells and shadows. The house had three main rooms and two side rooms. The three main rooms included two bedrooms in which Fourth Wife You and Third Daughter each had a bed. Of the two side rooms, one was a kitchen and the other was Fourth Idiot's bedroom. The window in the latter bedroom had a wooden frame that was built right into the wall. When one of her children had an episode, Fourth Wife You would lock them up in this prison-like room. The door was two inches thick and was made from a combination of ash and persimmon wood. When the door was locked from the outside, there was absolutely no way of opening it from the inside.

Fourth Wife You locked Fourth Idiot up in this room. He climbed to the window like an aggrieved criminal and began shouting, "Ma, Ma! I didn't have an episode. My mind is completely clear. I won't touch my sister's nipples anymore, OK?" Fourth Wife You ignored him, and instead changed into a freshly washed fluorescent blue shirt and combed her hair with a wooden comb. She removed several cold buns and placed them on the kitchen counter, then put half a bowl of noodles on the corner of the stove. Finally, she brought Third Daughter over to the kitchen doorway, pointed, and said, "Your mother is going to find you a family to marry into. At noon you can cook a bowl of noodles, and you and your brother can each have two steamed buns. You can hand your brother a bowl of noodles through the window."

Fourth Wife You asked, "Can you do that?"

Third Daughter replied, "Yes, I can." Then she added, "Ma, find me a good family to marry into. Find me a wholer."

Without another word, Fourth Wife You went into the courtyard, collected half a bowl of crushed rocks, then handed the bowl to Fourth Idiot through the window, saying, "Count these rocks. If you count them right, I'll let you out. If you count them wrong, you can continue stewing inside." Then she walked out into the street.

She passed a middle-aged woman nursing an infant. "Fourth Wife You, where are you headed on such an important day?"

Fourth Wife You replied, "A relative is sick, and I'm going to visit."

The woman asked, "But aren't you planting wheat? It's important to plant the wheat."

Fourth Wife You replied, "My relative's illness is terminal, so I really need to go, even if it means not planting the wheat."

Fourth Wife You didn't tell the woman that she was actually trying to find a family for her daughter to marry into. Her four idiot children had made her infamous throughout the Balou Mountains. No one in the neighboring villages called You Village by its actual name; they all called it Four Idiots Village. The residents of You Village complained that those from other villages were rude and that Fourth Wife You had ruined their village's reputation. Several years earlier, when Fourth Wife You was looking for husbands for her two elder daughters, the villagers leaked the secret of her daughters' illness, and no one would have them. Fourth Wife You had stood at the eastern edge of the village and shouted at the top of her lungs,

"Hey . . . I want everyone to listen carefully . . . I'll fuck your ancestors, I'll dig up their graves. You're trying to keep my two elder daughters from finding husbands. You told everyone that my family is full of idiots, but when did this family of idiots ever keep you from screwing around, or keep your elders from kicking the bucket? Now, everyone listen to me . . . from this point onward, my children will marry whomever they choose, and whoever says otherwise will get sores in their mouths, run pus from their gums, get cancer of the throat, and after they die their graves will be dug up by grave robbers and their bones will be left out to be devoured by wild animals!"

Fourth Wife You moved to a pile of shit in the center of the village and cursed, then to a tree stump on the western side of the village and continued to curse. She cursed in all directions as she walked from one end of the village to the other. The door to every house was open, and people's heads popped out like eggplants along the edge of the fields. But by the time she finished cursing at the western end of the village, and turned around to head back, the doors of every house were tightly shut, and the street was completely empty. The chickens and pigs were so terrified that they cowered in nooks and crannies.

Half a year later, the two elder daughters moved out of Fourth Wife You's home and into those of their respective husbands. Eldest Daughter's husband was a cripple who walked with a cane and had to lean on his bed when he wanted to go to sleep. Second Daughter's husband, meanwhile, had a bad eye, which was always covered with a yellowish film as though it hadn't been washed properly. Before the marriage, both men asked Fourth Wife You if her daughters were really cured, and she said, "Yes, and if you don't believe me, go ask around the village." They did so, and the villagers all said they hadn't heard that Fourth Wife You's children were sick, and even if they had been sick when they were younger, they were better now.

The cripple married Eldest Daughter in the latter half of that year. It was snowing hard on the day of the wedding, and after their marriage, their lives were dark and cold. By contrast, the one-eyed man married Second Daughter at the start of spring in the following year. The sun was shining brightly on the day of the wedding, and the wind was blowing down from the mountain ridge like a sheet of silk. Their lives, however, stumbled along. On the first night of her marriage, Second Daughter had an episode and began foaming at the mouth. At the time, One-Eye happened to be in bed with her, and afterward each time they tried to sleep together her illness would act up, and she constantly had to take medication. The summer after Second Daughter was married off, Fourth Wife You went to visit her son-in-law's home. Her village was located thirty-nine *li* from that of her son-in-law, but before she had gone ten *li* she heard her daughter crying after having to take her medicine. When she arrived at their house, she found a pile of empty medicine bottles so high it reached the window ledge.

She asked One-Eye, "If she gets sick every time you try to sleep with her, couldn't you simply not sleep with her?"

One-Eye replied, "I didn't get married until I was already thirty-seven, and if I can't sleep with my wife, then why did I get married at all? If I can't sleep with my wife, how will my family name live on?"

After that, Fourth Wife You never returned to the home of her second son-in-law, and she rarely visited that of her first son-in-law either. As a result, she didn't know whether or not her daughters' illnesses were still acting up, nor whether Second Daughter ever ended up getting pregnant. Originally, Fourth Wife You had planned to visit her two daughters after the autumn harvest, but then the problem of her Third Daughter's marriage presented itself.

The mountain ridge was vast and endless. The wind brought in surge after surge of the smell of freshly turned earth. Sometimes, Fourth Wife You would pass people going to the market beyond the Balou Mountains. Both of Fourth Wife You's elder daughters had married into families who lived beyond the mountains. Outsiders were normally not willing to marry women from the mountains, feeling that a visit to the in-laws would be too much work. This was even more true of the Yous, whose idiot children could only look to the deep hills for mates. Fourth Wife You walked quickly as the sun's shadows fluttered around her like black veils. Li Village, Liu Gully, and both Large and Small Scholar Town were now all behind her, like discarded sheets of paper strewn across the sunlit hills. She proceeded alone, accompanied by the sound of countless sparrows and grasshoppers. In the afternoon, after the sun had passed its highest point, she heard footsteps slowly approaching, like an old person clapping. The sound faded into the distance, and she lifted her head to see if she could figure out exactly what the footsteps sounded like, whereupon she discovered that her husband, Stone You, was following her. She asked, "Where are you going?"

He replied, "If you keep going west to Wu Ravine, you'll find five brothers who are all bachelors, any one of whom would make a match for Third Daughter."

Fourth Wife You stopped and looked at her husband skeptically. She noticed that a mosquito had landed on his left cheek, so she swatted it away and proceeded forward. When she reached an intersection, she stood there uncertainly, and her husband said, "You should take the road heading west." So, she took the road heading west, and soon saw Wu Ravine Village in front of her. The village was not very large, only a hundred or so residents. In front of the village there were several villagers busy harvesting the corn and planting wheat. Because she was so dressed up and was walking so quickly, the villagers all stopped what they were doing and stared at her. One of her sisters recognized her from a distance. The woman's family was large, with many children and grandchildren, and the three generations were out in the fields planting wheat. They held their hands up to their foreheads to block the glare of the sun as they looked at her. Suddenly, the woman pulling one of the plow's side ropes threw the rope down.

The woman's son-in-law asked, "Ma, what are you doing?"

The woman replied, "That's one of my sisters from when I still lived with my mother."

Stone You pulled Fourth Wife You to the entrance of the village and told her to wait there for a moment.

When the woman came over, she shouted, "Hey, are you my younger sister?"

Fourth Wife You called out in surprise, "Sis . . . it's you!"

The woman said, "This is such a busy time of year. How is it that you've come all the way here?"

Fourth Wife You said, "I've come to find a husband for Third Daughter. I hear that in your village there is a family with five sons, none of whom has a wife."

They stood there on the side of the road, staring at each other. After a while, their eyes filled with tears. As girls, they had gone together into the fields to fetch water and take the cattle out to graze, but after they each married they rarely had a chance to see each other. The woman was only about half a year older than Fourth Wife You, but looked as though she were more than a decade older, and had endured hardships that Fourth Wife You could only imagine. The woman had only just turned sixty, and was already walking unsteadily and had a face full of wrinkles. Fourth Wife You watched her, and said, "Sis, you're old, and have gone completely gray." The other woman replied, "You've also aged. I heard that before you even turned thirty, you were widowed with four children. I always said that I wanted to visit you and your children, but could never seem to find the time." Fourth Wife You asked, "How are your grandchildren doing? I hear you replaced your house with a tile-roofed one. I couldn't leave my children alone, or else I'd have come to help cook for you while you were building your new house."

The woman stared at her in surprise, and asked, "Then who's looking after Third Daughter and Fourth Idiot now, while you're here?"

Fourth Wife You replied, "I locked Fourth Idiot in his room."

The two sisters chatted there at the head of the field, until the tractor came rumbling over and the old man in the cabin urged them to return home. Only then did it occur to them that they should start heading back.

When they entered the village, Fourth Wife You saw that her sister did indeed have a new tile-roofed house with a courtyard—a house so new that the smell of sulfur from the bricks still lingered. The path through the courtyard and the ailanthus tree in the center were still enveloped in waves of dust from the new tiles. Under the tree, Fourth Wife You complimented her sister on how big and bright the new building was, how straight its girders were, how good its wood was, and she told her sister how much she envied her good life. Eventually, she broached the topic that had brought her there, revealing countless shameful details about Third Daughter and Fourth Idiot. The other woman lit a fire, rinsed some vegetables, kneaded some dough, and boiled some water. Then she went to a house in the back of the village and, in the blink of an eye, had summoned the eldest of the five sons. He was almost forty years old, and was thin and hunchbacked. When he heard that there was someone who wanted to marry her daughter to one of the brothers, he entered the room smiling brightly. He brought fresh dates, and invited Fourth Wife You to sit under the ailanthus tree and eat the dates as they chatted about the crops, the harvest, the drought, the house, and countless other topics.

Fourth Wife You asked, "So, none of you are married?"

The eldest son bowed his head and replied, "No, we're not."

Fourth Wife You said, "My daughter is twenty-eight years old, by the lunar calendar."

Eldest Brother replied, "In my family, Second Brother is thirty-five, Third Brother is thirty-three, Fourth Brother is thirty, and Fifth Brother is only twenty-seven."

Stone You said, "Either Second Brother or Third Brother would be fine."

Fourth Wife You said, "I think it would be best to have my daughter marry Fourth Brother, since the two of them are closest in age."

Eldest Brother replied, "Of the five of us, Fourth Brother is definitely the most handsome. He is trained as a carpenter, and a matchmaker has already offered to set him up with a young woman from a neighboring village."

Fourth Wife You asked, "How about Third Brother?"

Eldest Brother said, "Third Aunt mentioned that your third daughter has epilepsy, but is not unattractive. I understand that she can work and cook, and can even sew. Our second brother is deaf, having lost his hearing as a result of a fireworks accident when he was young, but apart from that there's nothing wrong with him. Do you think your daughter could get engaged to Second Brother?"

Stone You said, "She and Second Brother would make a good match."

Fourth Wife You said, "That won't do. I want to find a wholer for Third Daughter to marry. If only I can find her a wholer, then our family wouldn't need any betrothal gifts. In fact, we'll even give the groom's family a dowry chest, a double bed made from ailanthus wood, and a bedding set, together with two sets of year-round men's clothing."

Stone You asked, "Can we really provide all that?"

Fourth Wife You replied, "Don't interfere."

Eldest Brother said, "That is certainly a lot of gifts. But my brothers are interested in marrying a wife, not just things."

Fourth Wife You said, "We would be willing to accept any of the brothers, except for the deaf one."

Eldest Brother stood up and was about to walk away. He said, "Even if we were to let our deaf brother marry your daughter, it would only be because we were doing Third Aunt a favor."

Fourth Wife You also stood up and said angrily, "Go on, leave. May you all remain single for the rest of your lives."

Stone You tried to pull Fourth Wife You aside, but she knocked his hand away. Eldest Brother stood there, unsure of what to do. He watched as his third aunt walked out of the kitchen. Fourth Wife You turned around and walked briskly toward the courtyard entrance. In the street there were many villagers who had just got off work, and everyone looked at her and urged her to return to at least have lunch before leaving. She, however, merely stared back at Eldest Brother, who was left standing stock-still in the courtyard of the tile-roofed house. She repeated, "Other than the deaf one, can we marry any of the others?" Seeing Eldest Brother shake his head, she walked away.

She left behind a table full of food.

Chapter Three

By this point, the sun was already high in the sky and a thin mist was rising out of the mountain ridge. In the distance, the smoke from Wu Ravine Village gradually dissipated. Fourth Wife You ate some grain, drank some spring water, then followed Stone You's directions and visited several other villages. There, she met a number of men, but either they didn't want Third Daughter because of her illness, or else Fourth Wife You didn't want *them* because they were not wholers. She walked so far that her entire body ached, but in the end she couldn't find a husband for her daughter. She headed back toward the Balou Mountains, and on the way drew near Eldest Daughter's village. From a distance, she saw Elder Daughter's husband hobbling around in their apple orchard, irrigating the trees. He was alone, and in the empty mountain range he resembled a three-legged ox plowing the fields. Fourth Wife You's tears began streaming out.

Stone You asked, "What's wrong?"

She said, "I'll find Third Daughter a husband if it kills me."

Proceeding along the mountain path in the direction of Eldest Daughter's village, she saw clearly her daughter's twin caves, straw stove, and an apple orchard with no apples. The orchard represented the family's hopes and dreams, and after they planted the sprouts several years earlier, Eldest Daughter's crippled husband irrigated them, caring for them as though they were his own children. Eldest Daughter mended her husband's clothing, cooked food, and waited for those sprouts to grow into trees and begin producing fruit. But after three years, all of their neighbors' fruit trees were full of red blossoms, while her family's had only a few green sprouts without a trace of red. The following year, the trees in every other orchard were heavy with fruit, while her family's had just a few green apples that were as small as dates. As every other family was madly selling their fruit, Eldest Daughter had a nervous breakdown. She rushed into the orchard and began cursing her husband, saying, "You promised me that if we planted apple trees, within three years we would have enough money to buy me a colorful new shirt. I want that new shirt!" Cripple sat under a tree and stared into space, despair etched into the mountain-like ridges on his face. He became increasingly distressed by his wife's shouts, and suddenly lifted one of his crutches and violently brought it back down again. Eldest Daughter's head began bleeding and her mouth began foaming, whereupon she fell to the ground unconscious.

At that point, Fourth Wife You was out in the field picking beans. Her husband, Stone You, rushed over and told her what had happened. She immediately went to her daughter's house, several dozen *li* away. When she arrived in their courtyard, she saw that Cripple was in the process of chopping down the fruit trees, and one entire hillside was already stripped bare. Fourth Wife You rushed up to him and asked, "Are you crazy?"

Cripple responded, "Even our fruit trees won't bear fruit; I simply can't endure it anymore."

Fourth Wife You asked, "Did you use the same sprouts as everyone else?"

Cripple replied, "I bought them from the nursery."

She asked, "Did you use pesticide?"

Cripple replied, "These trees didn't have any insects to begin with."

She asked, "Did you graft them with a different strain?"

Cripple asked, "What do you mean?"

She explained, "I notice that other people first plant seedlings, and then the following year they ask someone to graft them."

Cripple stared at his chopped-down trees, then he dropped his ax and began slapping his own face, exclaiming, "My legs are stunted, but how is it that my mind is also stunted? My legs are crippled, but how is it that my mind is also crippled?" He stared up into the sky and began raving, "How could I not know that I needed to graft them? How could I not know?" He collapsed and, like Eldest Daughter, lay unconscious in the middle of the orchard.

The life of Eldest Daughter's family was a dark alley, and although they could occasionally discern a light at the end, it nevertheless seemed that they could never make their way out. Eldest Daughter and her husband had planted another crop of fruit trees, and Cripple cared for the seedlings as though they were his own children. The seedlings produced green sprouts, and at the beginning of the year Eldest Daughter and her husband performed a graft. But, though that year apples were as plentiful as sweet potatoes, they weren't able to sell a single one of theirs. Even though he wasn't able to sell his apples, Cripple nevertheless hobbled down to the river to fetch water to irrigate his crops, as if he planted fruit trees and fetched water for some purpose other than earning money.

When Stone You passed by that orchard, he saw Cripple carrying the water up the hill, and the shrimp that had jumped out of the bucket were crawling on the dry hillside. Stone You stood there watching from a distance, his hand to his forehead to shield his eyes from the sun. His face looked deathly pale.

Stone You said, "Let's go and have a word with our son-in-law."

Fourth Wife You replied, "What is there to say? He has a wife and an orchard. Eldest Daughter has a husband and food to cook. They have everything they need, and their lives are infinitely better than those of Third Daughter and Fourth Idiot."

Saying this, Fourth Wife You hurried off toward Wu Village several *li* away. Stone You noted that someone's wife in Wu Village had passed away about six months earlier, and he thought maybe she'd died just so her husband could marry Third Daughter. By this point, the sun was already low in the west and the mountain ridge was shrouded in a red glow. The autumn warmth washed over their feet like water. There was a scent of fresh earth, and the smell of grass filled the air. As though walking along a tightrope, they went down a small path overrun with weeds, followed by a flock of sparrows. They passed one ridge after another, as they proceeded down to the bottom of a ravine. Fourth Wife You saw many villagers speaking with her husband, but most of them were old people herding their sheep and oxen back to the village. There was a woman wearing a black silk shirt with the character for "Longevity" stitched on the back, who asked Stone You how to get to the Li Temple Primary School. Fourth Wife You asked, "She's not that old, is she?" Stone You replied, "This is the wife of that man from Wu Village. She was only thirty when she died in a cart accident."

Fourth Wife You paused and examined the woman. She saw that she was somewhat bowlegged and wobbled a bit with each step. Fourth Wife You heard the woman walking over, as soft as settling dust. She thought what a shame it was to pass away at such a young age. At this point, the woman turned around and, looking at her wanly, said, "Are the two of you going to Wu Village? My husband is a good-for-nothing who is only interested in eating, and is never willing to do any work. Now that I'm gone, he leads a completely joyless existence. As long as you can provide him with enough to eat and drink, he will surely agree to your marriage proposal."

Fourth Wife You stared at the woman in astonishment.

The woman nodded to Fourth Wife You, then appeared to float away.

They continued forward. The setting sun before them made a faint swishing sound. They followed the river for a while until a village appeared on the hillside. At several points along the path to the village, there were wooden signs bearing the names of the owner of the land. On some of the signs there also appeared, in small characters, the words THIS LAND IS UNDER CONTRACT, AND WILL REMAIN SO FOR FIFTY YEARS, WITHOUT CHANGE or IF ANYONE'S LIVESTOCK VENTURES ONTO THIS LAND, THAT PERSON'S FAMILY CAN EXPECT TO DIE! The wheat planted here had all been harvested, leaving row upon row of tracks where the wheat had been dragged through the field. You could also see the grain kernels that had not been buried, shimmering in the sunlight. Fourth Wife You and her husband came over from the recently harvested field and gazed out at the village in front of them. They could smell the evening air, and could see people in the village staring back at them.

Fourth Wife You asked, "Do you know the man's name and where he lives?"

Stone You replied, "I do. His name is Wu Shu, and he lives under the date tree in the center of the village. As long as someone is willing to marry Third Daughter, you shouldn't be too picky about other details."

Fourth Wife You replied angrily, "I don't care if it's his second marriage, but I definitely want him to be a wholer."

Stone You said, "So what if he's a bit disabled? We've already visited five villages and seen seven men; any of them would be fine for her."

Fourth Wife You stopped abruptly to look at her husband, and asked, "Have you gone to see how Eldest Daughter and Second Daughter are doing? Their pigs won't litter, their chickens won't lay eggs, and they themselves are not getting pregnant—there is not a single thing that does not give cause for worry. If our daughters had married wholers, would they have had a problem with their apple trees not bearing fruit? Would Second Daughter have been so frustrated with not being able to get pregnant that she would eventually resort to swallowing poison? Would they have been unable to wake up when it was time to harvest the crops?" As Fourth Wife You pummeled her husband with questions, he bowed his head and slowed down, such that he was now walking behind her. He didn't say a word, while Fourth Wife You continued muttering to herself. When they reached the village, they saw that in front there was a large empty field, about two or three *mu* in size, shaped like a cross between a circle and a square. The corn from the previous season had been swallowed up by weeds, and all that was left were a few bare stalks, which made the land appear more overgrown than it actually was. Wormwood, sawtooth, and twitch grass were all growing haphazardly in the field, to the point that someone standing beside it would have difficulty seeing the ground underneath. It was on the edge of that overgrown field that a man was sitting on a hoe and leaning against a pagoda tree. A fly had landed on his face, but he didn't bother to brush it away. They could see that his face was covered in the ash-gray pallor of the abandoned field, and it looked as if he were on the verge of death. As he heard someone approaching, he opened his eyes then immediately closed them again, as if he were completely exhausted.

Fourth Wife You said, "Hey, it's time for dinner. Is this Wu Village?"

The man grunted without looking around.

Fourth Wife You asked again, "Do you know where we can find Wu Shu's home?"

The man suddenly opened his eyes and stared at Fourth Wife You, and asked, "Why are you looking for Wu Shu?"

Stone You said, "This is Wu Shu."

Fourth Wife You examined the man and saw that his disheveled hair was full of straw and crawling with lice. His sleeves were torn, revealing inner arms covered in a layer of black dirt, and his black pants had dark blue patches sewn on the bottom with white thread. She also noticed he was wearing one old handmade cloth shoe and one new canvas-and-rubber one. Fourth Wife You asked, "Are you Wu Shu?"

The man chuckled and said, "I knew that you would come to see me. Today I saw a ghost, who told me that when the sun set someone would come and see me, and, sure enough, someone has now come."

Fourth Wife You said, "Please lift your arm."

Wu Shu hesitated a moment, then raised his arm.

Fourth Wife You said, "Roll up your pant legs."

Wu Shu did so, revealing a pair of calves that were as thick as tree trunks.

Fourth Wife You said, "You're not sick, are you?"

Wu Shu said, "What do you mean, sick?"

Fourth Wife You said, "Like deaf, mute, or mentally disabled."

Wu Shu said, "Don't you see me sitting here in front of you? I'm a wholer."

Fourth Wife You said, "Let me see you take a few steps."

Wu Shu stepped out from under the pagoda tree and walked back and forth in front of her. She saw that he had a nimble gait, his arms and legs looked strong, and he appeared happy. She thought, *Third Daughter has had good fortune. We've found a wholer.* He stood in front of her, his body as straight as a rod, and asked, "What else would you like to see?"

Fourth Wife You said, "How many houses does your family own?"

Wu Shu said, "A three-room thatched house, which leaks when it rains."

Fourth Wife You said, "That's not a problem. Do you own any fruit trees?"

Wu Shu said, "After my wife died, I sold all of my trees to buy food." He gestured toward a pagoda tree with a trunk as wide as a bowl, and said, "The day before yesterday, I gave this one to a neighbor in exchange for a basket of wheat, and in a few days he will come to chop it down."

Fourth Wife You said, "You don't raise chickens or pigs?"

Wu Shu replied, "If I don't even have enough food for myself?"

Fourth Wife You said, "Did you sew the patches on your clothing yourself?"

Wu Shu replied, "If I didn't do it, who would?"

Fourth Wife You said, "Do you also cook your own food?"

Wu Shu replied, "If I didn't cook it, who would?"

Fourth Wife You said, "How about if I find you someone to mend your clothing and cook for you?"

Wu Shu replied, "Do you mean your family's third daughter?"

Fourth Wife You stared in surprise, and said, "You already know everything?"

Wu Shu replied, "I really did see a ghost."

Stone You said, "Was it your wife who told you everything?"

Wu Shu asked, "So, what's the story with her illness?"

Fourth Wife You said, "It doesn't act up more than once every ten days or two weeks, and sometimes she'll go for a whole half year without a single episode."

Wu Shu looked upward, as though considering something.

Fourth Wife You said, "Maybe after you and she get married, her illness will be cured. That is what happened with our eldest two daughters. Their illness was as bad as a stormy day, but as soon as they got married the rain clouds cleared."

Wu Shu said, "And if it isn't cured?"

Fourth Wife You said, "It will be. Just marry her, and you'll see."

Wu Shu was silent for a long time. Then he straightened his neck and glanced at Fourth Wife You, saying, "If you want me to marry your family's third daughter, that's fine, but your family should add something extra to the dowry."

Fourth Wife You asked, "What do you want?"

Wu Shu said, "A dowry chest, including three sets of bedding with new covers and new cotton stuffing."

Fourth Wife You said, "Done."

Wu Shu said, "I'd also like five pairs of cloth shoes. I don't have any shoes to wear, and don't have any clothing either."

Fourth Wife You said, "I'll give you eight pairs of cloth shoes, two pairs of rubber shoes, and I'll also buy you two wool jackets."

Wu Shu said, "Can you also re-thatch the roof on our house?"

Fourth Wife You replied, "That wouldn't cost very much."

Wu Shu said, "Also buy me an ox." Looking out at the barren field next to his house, he added, "Hoeing this field by hand every year is exhausting."

Fourth Wife You hesitated, and asked, "How much does an ox cost?"

Wu Shu said, "I wouldn't need it immediately, so if I receive it within six months of the marriage, that would be fine."

Fourth Wife You said, "OK, in that case let's add an ox."

Stone You rushed in and shouted, "Are you crazy? Even if we were to sell everything we own, we still wouldn't have enough to buy an ox."

Fourth Wife You said, "I'm just trying to find a wholer."

Her husband said, "This wholer is a thief who is robbing you blind."

Fourth Wife You repeated, "I'm just trying to find Third Daughter a wholer."

Wu Shu asked, "Who are you talking to?"

Fourth Wife You said, "How about if you get married after planting the wheat?"

Wu Shu said, "My fields have been barren for a year, and I don't have a single seed to plant. You need to give me half of your family's corn and wheat crop, and also help me hoe my fields and plant my grain."

Stone You said, "You're trying to take advantage of my family, aren't you?"

Fourth Wife You said, "When we come to help hoe the fields, we'll also bring fertilizer and wheat seeds."

Stone You said, "I'd rather Third Daughter was dead than have her marry this type of greedy man. Are you trying to push our daughter into a fire?"

Fourth Wife You said, "As long as she can get married, she'll be fine. Many people are a total mess, but after they get married they become diligent and frugal."

Wu Shu looked around, then turned to Fourth Wife You and said, "I keep hearing someone twittering next to me. Look at that grass there—it used to be straight and tall but now someone has stomped it flat."

Fourth Wife You glanced down at the patch of grass, and said, "If you marry Third Daughter, will you treat her well?"

Wu Shu straightened his neck, and said, "How could I not treat my own wife well?"

Fourth Wife You proceeded to arrange her daughter's marriage as though she were completing a business transaction in which both parties were left satisfied. Then the bright red sun set behind the mountains, bathing the village's houses, trees, and streets in a purple glow, like a strange summer cloud.

Chapter Four

Autumn was over.

Many families had already sown their winter wheat.

It was during this period that Fourth Wife You planned to marry Third Daughter to the man from Wu Village, forty-five *li* away. She carried new thatching from her own village to her future son-in-law's house to help fix his leaky roof. She even stayed there and hoed several *mu* of barren soil. She collected all of the weeds and flower stems, together with the rocks and tiles that were mixed in with the soil, and piled them up along the edge of the field. Everything her son-in-law had requested was prepared to order, and the only thing left was for him to come and haul away half of their autumn harvest. The first time he came had been for the grain that was Third Daughter's dowry, and the second time would be for the grain she would eat after moving into her new home.

When Wu Shu first arrived, it was the third day of the lunar year, and they all woke at the crack of dawn. As soon as the sun came up, Wu Shu hauled a cart to the You family's front door. It was Third Daughter who went to open the door, and when she saw Wu Shu her eyes lit up with delight. Several days earlier, when she first realized that Wu Shu was a wholer, she hid in her room and refused to come out. Alone in her room, however, she laughed to herself. When Wu Shu left her home that time, she escorted him to the mountain peak and then returned, and that entire night she sat next to her bed chortling happily, refusing to lie down and go to sleep.

This time when she saw Wu Shu, Third Daughter was very friendly, and her blush of embarrassment disappeared like storm clouds on a clear day. She turned toward the main room and called out, "Ma, he's here," then proceeded into the kitchen, where she fried him an egg and brought it out.

Like a pear tree that bursts into bloom overnight, Third Daughter's illness was suddenly cured—and apart from sounding a bit manic when she laughed, and the fact that the stitches on the shoes she made for Wu Shu were somewhat too large, there was nothing about her that was out of the ordinary. On the other hand, Fourth Idiot's illness had become more and more acute. As soon as he learned that Third Daughter had gotten engaged and would be married, he kicked the door for several days straight, refusing to eat or speak. When Fourth Idiot saw Third Daughter, he began sobbing. His snot ran all the way down his neck, but he wouldn't even reach up to wipe it. It was as though he would lose something when Third Daughter got married.

Wu Shu ate his fried egg and wiped his mouth. When he handed his bowl back to Third Daughter, he pinched her mountain-like breasts, but she just laughed and stepped aside. When Fourth Idiot saw this, his face turned scarlet. He stood in the courtyard staring angrily at Wu Shu, his hands curled into fists as though he were about to rush forward and beat him.

Wu Shu stepped back half a step, then said, "I'm your brother-in-law, and your third sister is my wife."

Fourth Idiot cried out, "You're a pig, a dog, an ass!"

Third Daughter shouted, "Ma, your fourth son won't let me get married! Are you going to fix this?"

At that moment, Fourth Wife You was in her room packing up the several pairs of new shoes she had made for Wu Shu. She carefully threaded each pair together, then wrapped them in cloth. When she emerged, she stood under the awning and told Fourth Idiot to come over, saying that she wanted to tell him a secret. When he hesitantly approached, she slapped him and then pushed him inside his room and locked the door.

Fourth Idiot wailed, "I want a wife. I want to get married, too! I want to marry a wholer wife." At this point, the sun was shining down on the courtyard, and Fourth Idiot's cries, tears, and snot were illuminated by the sunlight streaming in through the window, as though a handkerchief used to wipe away tears had been hung out to dry.

Wu Shu said, "I don't know if joining this family was auspicious or not."

Fourth Wife You said, "You are marrying our third daughter, not our son. Quick, go load your grain onto the cart."

Wu Shu said, "I want to take some more."

Fourth Wife You said, "Take as much as you are able to haul away."

He parked the cart in the doorway and tied a rope to the end. He took sack after sack out of the cart, then opened the jar beneath the bed and began filling the sacks with the grain that was stored there. Fourth Wife You held the sacks open as Wu Shu used a basin to ladle the grain out of the jar. The entire room was filled with the sound of grain rubbing against the side of the basin. The scent of wheat had accumulated over the years like water behind a dam, lingering thickly in the room. Wu Shu filled one sack after another, and after each one was filled, he would pick it up and shake it a bit to let the grain settle to the bottom, so that he could then stuff in another couple of bowls. After Wu Shu filled the third sack, Third Daughter suddenly appeared from the kitchen with a rolling pin, and as he was stuffing grain into the sack, she used the rolling pin to stuff it down further. In this way, a sack that was usually able to hold twelve or thirteen bowls of grain could now hold fifteen.

Upon tying up the sack, Wu Shu looked at Fourth Wife You and laughed. "Third Daughter is not stupid at all."

Fourth Wife You replied, "Load it up, take as much as you can. As long as you treat her well and don't beat or curse her, it's OK."

Wu Shu said, "How could I do otherwise? For better or worse, she's now my wife. After all, a crazy person is still a person."

At this point, shouts could be heard coming from inside the house: "Good news! Your second son-in-law has arrived!" At first she couldn't believe it, but then she listened more carefully and sure enough, Second Son-in-Law had arrived. Fourth Wife You felt oddly anxious and hurried outside to take a look. Her son-in-law was strolling up from the village entrance. In the sunlight, he stood as big and strong as a century-old tree, and each time he took a step, a cloud of dust swirled up from under his feet. Fourth Wife You thought to herself that his arrival must mean something, since it had been several years since he last visited. As he approached, Fourth Wife You couldn't discern anything out of the ordinary from his expression; there was only a glint of happiness in his one good eye. She said, "You've arrived! What about Second Daughter?"

He stopped in front of the main gate and replied with a smile, "She's at home resting. We think she may be pregnant, as she has suddenly developed a craving for sour and spicy foods."

Fourth Wife You's heart jumped for joy, and she asked, "Do you need anything?"

He replied, "No, nothing in particular."

Fourth Wife You said, "If there is anything you need, just let me know."

Her son-in-law sat on her doorstep and said, "I don't need anything."

Fourth Wife You said, "Then why don't you go home and rest? If you want to eat something, I'll fix it for you."

Second Son-in-Law loosened his collar, wiped the sweat from his brow, and said, "I already had breakfast at home. Second Daughter cooked me a fried bun."

Fourth Wife You said, "She can cook fried buns? You should go and meet with Third Son-in-Law."

Second Son-in-Law's hand froze as he was wiping his brow. He looked at the cart in the entranceway, and asked, "Has he come to claim some grain?"

Fourth Wife You said, "Let him. Do you need any?"

Second Son-in-Law said, "We don't need any grain, but there is something else I want."

A cloud passed over Fourth Wife You's face. She pulled aside her graying hair and said, "Just tell me what you need."

Second Son-in-Law stood up. He was silent for a moment, then stuttered that now that Second Daughter was pregnant, her illness had been acting up again, and in the past month she had had several more episodes. In fact, she had had two episodes the day before—the first occurred when she was leaning over the cistern to ladle out some water for cooking. She suddenly cried out in pain and with a *thunk* fell into the cistern. When the second episode occurred, she collapsed on the well platform and nearly fell into the well and drowned. When Second Son-in-Law finished telling this to Fourth Wife You, he gazed ahead at the village and asked, "What are we going to do? What in the world are we going to do? It was hard enough for her to get pregnant in the first place." Four Idiots Village was located on a mountainside, and there were old straw mats hanging everywhere. The villagers living downhill all emerged from the village's streets and alleys, herding sheep and carrying shovels and scythes; as they disappeared into the distance, the sparkling dust on their bodies gradually melted into the light from the distant fields. Second Son-in-Law looked back at Fourth Wife You, and pleaded, "If Second Daughter is not able to have this child, I don't even want to live."

Fourth Wife You said, "Tell me what you need."

Second Son-in-Law said, "Every night, I dream I'm running around to find an old Chinese medical practitioner. He tells me I should make her some bone marrow soup, which will cure her illness."

Fourth Wife You said, "Then make her some."

Second Son-in-Law said, "But the prescription doesn't call for just any kind of bones."

Fourth Wife You asked, "What kind of bones do you need?"

Second Son-in-Law hesitated, then said, "It calls for the bones of a dead person, a relative, and the closer the kin the better."

Fourth Wife You was silent for a while. She looked at her son-in-law's face, then over at the village. She turned toward her house, and from beneath the awning she pulled out a hoe and a couple of shovels. Standing in the courtyard, she shouted, "Third Daughter . . . Wu Shu . . . there is something I need to attend to. The two of you can take as much grain as you need. Go ahead and fill up the entire cart, since you've made the trip." Then, carrying the tools, she left the house. Second Son-in-Law was still standing there waiting. Fourth Wife You came over and handed him the hoe, then led him to the mountain ridge.

Second Son-in-Law asked in surprise, "Ma, where are you going?"

"To dig up the grave of Second Daughter's father," Fourth Wife You replied without turning around. "Didn't you say you needed a dead person's bones to cure Second Daughter's illness? I'll help get whatever you need."

Second Son-in-Law ran up to her, the color draining from his face, surprised at how quickly everything was progressing. He said, "I feel a bit bad about her father."

Fourth Wife You replied, "Her father is the one who should feel bad about us."

Second Son-in-Law said, "Even dead, he can't lie in peace."

Fourth Wife You replied, "He is the one who is not letting us live in peace." They walked quickly. Fourth Wife You was only a step away from sixty, but even carrying the shovel she was still faster than her thirty-year-old son-in-law.

Wheat sprouts already blanketed the entire field. The grave was located in a cemetery several *li* away, where each of the You family graves had a cypress or pine tree planted next to it, covering the ground in shade. The sunlight was squeezed by the shade into a variety of different shapes, or else simply remained shapeless. In front of Stone You's grave there was a mountain pine, and since Stone You had been dead for a long time, the pine tree had already grown quite tall and bore several sparrow nests. When they reached the grave, Second Son-in-Law hung his shirt on a branch and used a shovel to dig open the grave, knocking down many twigs, leaves, and pinecones in the process.

The grave was opened.

The warm soil emitted milky white steam that spiraled upward and mixed with the scent from the pine trees, the decayed odor of the casket, and the fragrant smell of wheat.

Second Son-in-Law tossed out spadeful after spadeful of soil, as Fourth Wife You waited under the pine tree and collected pine nuts. Several sparrows were sitting on the tree branches, singing as they looked down at the village before flying away. Another dozen or so sparrows came and alighted in the tree, their songs like a shower on a clear day.

Second Son-in-Law stood on his tiptoes and peeked out of the grave. "What are they twittering about?"

Fourth Wife You said, "Keep digging. They're a good omen—it means Second Daughter's illness really will be cured."

Second Son-in-Law opened the door to the tomb, and inside he found the decayed coffin. The black paint had long since peeled off, and the wood had been gnawed by insects into a dense honeycomb. The tomb was actually a cellar, and was half a normal person's height. He squatted in the opening of the tomb, and in the sunlight he could see that the coffin was resting on several large stones, and there were two white maggots crawling around on the lid. He knew that these were ordinary grubs, but the sound of them crawling was as though a mosquito had flown into his ear. The character for "Offering," inscribed on the lid of the coffin, was still faintly visible, and below it there was a date-sized opening that looked like a dark eye staring out. White smoke wafted from the opening, up past the door of the tomb and Second Son-in-Law's head. Second Son-in-Law squatted at the opening of the tomb, as though he had lost the keys to his house and was locked out. Fourth Wife You shouted down to him, "Are you afraid?" He replied, "Have I *ever* been afraid?" She said, "Then open the coffin," and he replied, "I was just about to." He ducked his head and shuffled forward a couple of steps, then placed his hands on the front of the coffin and gently shook it back and forth.

The coffin fell apart. There was the sound of decayed wood shattering, and a cloud of smoke surged out, like water vapor from a hot steamer.

After the dust and smoke dissipated, Second Son-in-Law stood there motionless. Not a speck was left of his father-in-law's flesh, and the clothing had completely disintegrated. Instead, there was just a layer of dust and a skeleton—foot bones, leg bones, hip bones, back bones, neck bones, and a skull, all neatly arranged in their original configuration. The skull resembled a sheet of dirty paper that had fallen to the ground in the middle of the night, while the two eyes were still clear and bright, like two wells sitting in the sunlight. A shiver ran down his spine, as he took two steps back and shouted,

"Ma . . . come take a look."

Fourth Wife You went down.

Second Son-in-Law said, "Say something to my father-in-law. Give him some sort of explanation."

Fourth Wife You said, "We are trying to cure his daughter's illness. There's nothing to explain." With this, she entered the tomb, squatted in front of the coffin and pushed aside a couple of maggots that had fallen onto the leg bones. She looked everything over and saw that, apart from some white moss, the walls of the tomb were completely intact. "Good soil in this tomb," she remarked. Then she turned and asked, "Did you bring a sack?"

Second Son-in-Law took a white cloth out of his pocket and laid it out in the lighted area at the entrance to the tomb.

Fourth Wife You asked, "Which bone do you want?"

Second Son-in-Law said, "Whenever Second Daughter has an episode, her hand begins to tremble, so let's take a bone from his hand."

Fourth Wife You took two bones from her husband's hand and placed them on the cloth, then asked, "What else?"

Second Son-in-Law said, "Whenever she has an episode, she loses the ability to walk."

Fourth Wife You took one of her husband's leg bones and placed it on the cloth, then asked, "What else?"

Second Son-in-Law said, "Anything is fine. Just take a few more."

Fourth Wife You said, "Mental illness is the result of something wrong in the brain, and if the brain can be fixed the illness will be cured. So, we should definitely use the skull." As she was saying this, she took the skull and held it in both hands as though it were a bowl, then gently placed it on the cloth. She tied up the four corners of the cloth, and after Second Son-in-Law climbed out of the grave, she handed him the bundle. Then she stepped out of the dirt hole and, holding Stone You's hand, left the graveyard.

Outside, the sun was already at its apex, shining down brightly as the trees and mountains twinkled in the sunlight. On the opposite hill, a villager was preparing his field for planting. He was standing on an elevated area and asked Fourth Wife You what she was doing at the graveyard. She replied that the grave of her husband, who had gone on to enjoy better days, had been flooded by the rain, and she and Second Son-in-Law had come to fill in the collapsed pit. The villager went back to preparing his soil, and the rhythmic sound of his work reverberated up the ravine to the riverbank opposite, and to the other side of the mountain ridge beyond.

After filling in the grave and replacing the grave mound, Fourth Wife You and Second Son-in-Law had picked up their tools and returned home. The bone-filled bundle was tied to the handle of Second Son-in-Law's spade, and it swung back and forth as he walked. All the while, the bones made a grinding sound like bright moonlight falling to Earth, and a stench of decay trailed silently under their feet. Along the mountain ridge, villagers were on their way home after a day's work. They were driving sheep and oxen, some villagers walking in front of the animals and others walking behind. Upon reaching the crossroad that turned to the village, Fourth Wife You asked, "What are we going to have for lunch? Garlic noodles?" Second Son-in-Law replied, "I'm not going. Let Third Son-in-Law eat there. I don't like him; he takes everything he wants just because he's a wholer."

Fourth Wife You said, "But it is still another several dozen *li* back to your house."

Second Son-in-Law replied, "I'm worried about Second Daughter home alone, with no one to take care of her if she has an episode."

Fourth Wife You took the hoe and the shovel from Second Son-in-Law and said, "You go ahead then."

Second Son-in-Law switched the bundle of bones to his other hand, and said, "I'm leaving."

He left, and in the blink of an eye, he and his bundle of bones disappeared into the mountain light.

Fourth Wife You continued standing there in the road watching him, and after he was out of sight she called out,

"Hey . . . you should treat Second Daughter well . . . be more compassionate with her . . ."

She heard his reply emerge from the yellow sunlight, "Ma . . . don't worry! After the baby is born, I'll bring you to live with us for a few days . . ."

Fourth Wife You returned home and was shocked by what she saw. Everything had been turned upside down. The courtyard was covered in spilled grain, and the ancestral tablet on a table in the main room had been toppled over. Stone You's portrait had fallen to the ground, and the curtains along the wall had been torn down. The grain jars in the interior room had all been opened, and the lids had been left strewn around the bed, the chest, and on the floor. Fourth Wife You went inside to take a look, and it was only then that she noticed that all of the jars were completely empty. Even the jar at the head of the bed, which had been filled with freshly ground flour, had been completely emptied out, and all that was left was a thin layer of flour on the bedding. As for the two *jin* of sesame oil that had been stored under the table, even the bottle itself was gone. She spun around and walked out, only to notice that there was a ladder leaning against the tree in the courtyard and the freshly picked ears of corn that had been hanging from the tree branches and the courtyard wall were also missing. Everything had been taken by that wholer, Third Son-in-Law.

It was as though they had been robbed. In the blink of an eye, all of the new and old grain was gone, together with the grain stored in a jar under the table. The corn in the courtyard and a sack of beans in the kitchen were also missing. Fourth Wife You stood stunned in the middle of the courtyard, staring at the bare tree branches and the courtyard wall. She felt her legs grow limp and almost collapsed. She managed to stagger forward a couple of steps, leaning against the tree branch on which they had previously hung corn to dry, then called out for Third Daughter, but there was no response. A deep silence flooded the courtyard, and swept over Fourth Wife You. She suddenly remembered Fourth Idiot, whom she had left locked up in his room. She quickly went up to look in through the window, and saw that he was sleeping soundly, with saliva dribbling out of his mouth. At the head of the bed, there was half a fried bun.

Fourth Wife You leaned against the window and shouted, "Pig! Will you wake up?"

Fourth Idiot woke up and sat up in bed.

Fourth Wife You asked him, "Where's Third Daughter?"

Fourth Idiot rubbed his eyes and said, "She left with her husband."

Fourth Wife You asked, "Where did they put all of our grain?"

Fourth Idiot said, "They hauled it away. I saw them load it onto their cart."

Fourth Wife You asked, "They were able to get it all on one cart?"

Fourth Idiot said, "After Third Daughter married her husband, that ass caressed her breasts in the courtyard, then she went into the village to help him borrow another cart. After that, they left—each of them hauling a cart full of grain."

Fourth Wife You felt her legs go limp, as though her bones had turned to rubber. She slid to the ground, where the midday sun beat down on her. Through the window, she heard Fourth Idiot chewing on his fried bun, and asked, "Fourth Babe, so you just watched as they hauled away all of our grain, and didn't do anything to stop them?"

Fourth Idiot replied, "They cooked me a fried bun—a scallion bun I never had before."

He added, "Ma, have you ever had a fried bun?" As he said this, a piece of fried bun fell from the window onto Fourth Wife You's head, and then dropped to the ground. She looked at the bun, which was round and had a bite taken out of it. She could make out every individual tooth mark. She focused her attention on the canine marks, and after staring for a while and resting a moment, she leaned against the wall and stood up. She retrieved a key from where it was hidden in the door-frame, opened the door, and let Fourth Idiot out.

Fourth Idiot walked out as though he had just been released from prison. He squinted in the sunlight, ran around the courtyard, and came to a stop in front of Fourth Wife You.

Fourth Wife You asked him, "Fourth Babe, do you think Third Sister's husband treats her well?"

Fourth Idiot said, "Yes, extremely well. They even hold hands when they go to the outhouse together."

Fourth Wife You said, "Now you and I are the only ones left. What do you want to eat?"

Fourth Idiot said, "I just had five fried buns, and now I'm thirsty." Fourth Wife You then told him that, now that Third Sister was gone, she wouldn't lock him up in his room anymore. Instead, she would go fix him a bowl of soup and boil him two cloves of pickled garlic.

Chapter Five

Night fell.

As night fell, the sky grew overcast. The mountain ridge behind the village dissolved into darkness like overcooked vegetables being boiled in a pot. The empty house suddenly appeared as desolate as an empty field at night. The grain was all gone, and two of the jars were shattered. Third Daughter and that wholer had even taken the string of chili peppers that had been hanging over the door. Also missing was a pagoda tree branch that had been cut to serve as a hoe handle, which had been leaning against the wall behind the door. Carrying an oil lamp, Fourth Wife You put Fourth Idiot to bed, then paced around her room several times. She wanted to clean up the house before going to sleep, but was so exhausted that she couldn't muster the energy to take another step.

So, she went directly to bed.

As she was about to fall asleep, Fourth Wife You heard a shadowy sound in the room, as though the wind were whispering to her. There was also the soft sound of footsteps pacing back and forth. At this point, the wind began to disperse the black clouds outside, and through the window they could be seen floating away like water pooled up along the riverbank. The clouds sounded like sparrows breathing. The darkness crowding in through the window piled up on the table and the bed, passed over the bedding and crawled up the wall. Fourth Wife You lay in bed with her eyes half-open, but after a while she suddenly heard the soft sound of sobbing coming from inside the house. She got up to take a look, and saw that it was her husband, Stone You, who was curled up in the darkness streaming in through the window, like an earthworm dried in the sun. She said, "You worthless thing, your daughter boils a few of your bones and suddenly you are left like this?"

He replied, "Now that the house has been emptied out, how are you and Fourth Idiot going to manage?"

She said, "We can still live in the house. We have a bed to sleep in and we still have land on the ridge, so we won't starve." She added, "You should move on, and in the future if you find yourself missing some bones or sinews and have difficulty walking, don't come looking for me. What good would it do to come to me? Can you help me plow the fields? Can you help me fetch water? Can you help me fetch a sack of someone's leftover grain?" He bowed his head so low it seemed as though his hair was draped over his feet. Outside the window, the clouds had already completely dispersed, and inside the house the moonlight cascaded down like water. As Stone You remained curled on the floor, Fourth Wife You returned to bed and said, "If you aren't going to leave, at least you can make yourself useful and help me clean the house. Tomorrow, I'm going to get up early to take out the night soil, and then you and I can go visit Eldest and Second Daughters."

Then, Fourth Wife You abruptly went to sleep.

The next day, she woke up at dawn and saw that the house was still a mess. The only change was that there were now two pools of wet tears in the spot where her husband, Stone You, had lain curled up in a ball all night. She looked over at the two wet patches and said to herself, *What's the point? I still need to do everything myself.* She righted the overturned jars, straightened the ancestral tablets, swept the floor, covered the two pools of tears, and took the night soil out into the fields.

Autumn had ended, and the frost had fallen. She cooked Fourth Idiot a fried bun and placed it at the head of his bed, then made a pot of watery soup and left it on the stove.

She took a couple of days to go visit her two daughters.

Second Daughter lived close by, so Fourth Wife You went to visit her first.

Second Daughter lived in a three-room adobe-walled house, and the courtyard was filled with tung trees that had already begun to shed their leaves. The ground was covered in river sand, and when they sprinkled water on the ground and swept up all the dirt and dust, the sand would sparkle in the sunlight. The courtyard walls were made of recently tamped earth, and stood straight and tall. There was a red glow in the air, and a fresh scent emanated from the courtyard, entrancing everyone as though it were early spring. Fourth Wife You thought that, as in previous years, she would be able to smell even from several *li* away the bitter scent of the Chinese medicines her daughter was brewing, and that after entering the village half the villagers would give her the cold shoulder on account of the fact that she had given birth to four idiot children and married her idiot daughter into this village. This time, they didn't. Instead, all of the villagers had gone into the fields, and the few familiar people Fourth Wife You did run into simply smiled and nodded to her. As she was walking down the street, at one point she stopped and stood in the sun in front of Second Daughter's courtyard. She stroked the smooth adobe walls, and looked up at the rows of small tiles lining the tops of the walls. She gently pushed open the door to enter the courtyard, and then stood there silently. The sand got into her shoes and made her feet itch. The steam from the ground had a fragrant smell. She went over to the window and saw that the medicine dregs that had been piled there were now gone, and instead there was a brown stone table surrounded by several stone benches. The sun was shining down, and Second Daughter was drying out the cloth shoe soles she had just sewn. Her daughter had her back to Fourth Wife You, and each time she sewed a stitch she would hold her hand in the air and look over to the right, then run the needle through her hair. Fourth Wife You stood quietly behind her daughter. She was surprised to see her daughter's hair neatly arranged in a thick braid without a single strand out of place. In thirty years, she had never seen her daughter's hair so tidy. Fourth Wife You's heart began to race with excitement. She saw that her daughter's face was bright red, like the leaves of a persimmon tree after a rainstorm. Her daughter could embroider and sew shoe soles—things she'd never been able to do before the marriage. Now, not only could she apparently do these things, but furthermore the soles she sewed were all tight and even, and on the bottoms she had embroidered a pattern like a woman's braids. Turning to the sewing kit on the stone table, Fourth Wife You saw that it was made from wicker and smelled of fresh paint. She turned to Second Daughter's neatly arranged clothes, and noticed that the stitching consisted of a single continuous thread—turning and going straight where necessary, like a path through a mountain range. At this point, Fourth Wife You couldn't help calling out to her daughter.

Second Daughter turned around, and the hand holding the thread froze in midair.

Fourth Wife You said, "Daughter."

Second Daughter put down her needle and thread, and immediately stood up. "Mother."

Mother and daughter gazed at one another, as the leaves from the tung tree in the courtyard gently fluttered to the ground.

Fourth Wife You asked, "You can make shoes?"

Second Daughter blushed, and said, "I want to make a pair of shoes for my brother."

Fourth Wife You asked, "Did you make the clothes you are wearing now?"

Second Daughter looked down at her clothes and replied, "Yes, I did."

Fourth Wife You said, "That sewing kit is also yours?"

Second Daughter said, "My husband just bought it for me—a home needs a sewing basket."

Fourth Wife You's eyes filled with tears. She remained silent for a long time, and then asked, "And what about your illness? Are you any better?"

Second Daughter began to sob silently, tears streaming down her face and onto her clothing. Her face, however, continued beaming, a glow of excitement emanating from her cheeks. She said, "Mother, I drank an entire cartload of that Chinese medicine, until the dregs were piled as high as a mound of night soil, but it didn't have any effect whatsoever. Last month, however, my husband brought back a bag of bones he found somewhere, and boiled them with some red dates and crystal sugar. After I drank the first dose I became so excited I couldn't sleep that night, and after the second I felt as though I could fly. Those bones yielded seven doses in all, and yesterday I finished the final one. After I drank the third dose, whenever other villagers saw me they said my illness seemed almost cured, and by the time I finished the sixth batch my husband said I no longer had the slightest trace of illness." As Second Daughter was saying this, her tears gradually dried, leaving behind only a glow of excitement. When she opened her mouth to speak, it was as if she were opening a sluice gate and letting the water pour out. As the sun began shining on the eastern side of the courtyard, her entire face was bathed in light, as red as though it had been painted. It didn't even occur to Second Daughter that her mother had walked several dozen *li* to visit her, and might need to sit down and have something to eat or drink. Instead, Second Daughter continued standing at a distance, chattering nonstop as though she had never before had a chance to speak with her mother. She said that after her illness was cured, she asked her husband countless times whose bones these were and where he had found them. She asked him to go fetch some more, so that her sisters and her brother could take the medicine as well, but her husband wouldn't say a word. Second Daughter said that her husband had taken several saplings to sell in the township. He had planned to buy a few things and then return, and afterward the two of them would go to her mother's house. She added that, before returning to visit her mother, she had planned to finish making this pair of shoes for her younger brother as part of her sisterly devotion to her idiot brother. At this point, Second Daughter picked up one of the shoes and examined it, noting that this one was already done and that she would finish the other one later that day. She would nail the straps on overnight, and then her younger brother would be able to wear the shoes she had made for him with her own hands. Fourth Wife You's tears began welling up and she suddenly doubled over, as though she had been standing for too long and needed to stop and rest. She squatted in front of her daughter and began wailing. She covered her face with her hands as tears streamed down. Her weary sobs became bright, as they flowed through Second Daughter's house and courtyard and out into the village and the mountain range. In the blink of an eye, the entire world was filled with the sound of weeping.

Second Daughter was startled. She stared at her mother, then rushed over and shouted, "Ma, what's wrong? What's wrong? Aren't you happy I'm cured?" She shook her mother's arm with both hands, until her mother almost toppled over. Upon hearing the ruckus, her neighbors came rushing over, as did people who were merely walking down the street. Soon, a large crowd was standing in the courtyard, and they all asked, "What's wrong?" Second Daughter replied, "When she saw I was cured, my mother started crying. And she cried so hard it seemed as though she were made of tears." One villager tried to comfort Fourth Wife You, saying, "It is a miracle your daughter's illness has been cured. Why would you cry over a miracle?" Another said, "Don't pressure her. Let her cry it out. She is crying from delight that her daughter is cured. Those are tears of happiness." So the villagers stopped trying to restrain her, and assumed she would eventually stop on her own. But she continued crying harder than ever, as long as the endless road through the fields. Eventually, the villagers got fed up, and one man said, "How are you still crying? What is there to cry about? Why don't we buy some more of the medicine your daughter took, and cure your other three children as well?"

With this, the man walked away.

Fourth Wife You stared silently at the man's departing shadow. She had a peaceful expression, beneath which there was a sudden burst of excitement. She looked out at her daughter's neighbors and said, "You can all leave now. I won't cry anymore. The You family has been saved." After the villagers all left, her excitement gradually faded and was replaced by a layer of pale determination, as though she were wearing a metal mask. She said, "Second Daughter, come here to mother." Then she squeezed her daughter's hand, pulled and stretched her arms, and peeled back her eyelids. She waved her hand in front of her daughter's face and saw that her large black eyes spun to follow her hand. Eventually, she asked, "Do you still fear your husband at night?"

Second Daughter blushed and said, "I am cured now."

Fourth Wife You said, "Give mother two bowls of egg noodle soup, and then mother will return home."

Second Daughter said, "Ma, why don't you sleep over tonight? Tomorrow my husband will return from town. He said that he was going to buy you a scarf."

Fourth Wife You replied, "I have to go home tonight. Now I know how to cure this illness. Give mother two bowls of soup, and I'll be on my way."

Second Daughter stood there with a look of surprise.

Fourth Wife You said, "Go on, and give me some extra eggs in the soup, and some extra sesame oil."

Chapter Six

Fourth Wife You left after lunch. By that point, the sky was high, the clouds were sparse, and vast fields of grain sprouts blanketed the mountains and ravines virtually overnight. There was a pungent odor in the air. Second Daughter escorted her mother to the mountain ridge, whereupon Fourth Wife You told her to return home. She said, "Go back. If you can find your brother a wholer wife, then you will have done your part as a sister. Don't think that simply making a pair of shoes will do it."

Second Daughter stood on the ridge as her mother disappeared into the distance. Fourth Wife You did not return to her Eldest Daughter's home. Along the mountain ridge she glanced in the direction of her Eldest Daughter's home and began to shout, "Daughter, Mother is leaving. Mother can cure you and your sisters." She watched as her shout drifted out through the mountain ridge like a piece of silk, then quickly headed home.

As Fourth Wife You proceeded through the mountain range, she felt the urge to talk to someone. When it occurred to her that her husband, Stone You, had not accompanied her to her Second Daughter's house, she felt a pang of loneliness. It was the first time in years that her husband had not accompanied her when she went on a trip. She wondered what was wrong with him. Now that he was no longer among the living, was it still possible for him to get sick? As she walked, she began to cry out, "Dead one, where are you? When I want you to talk to me, you really are dead; but when I don't want you to keep talking, you come back to life . . ." She shouted as she continued forward, at which point a man leading a plow ox approached from the opposite direction. He stopped and asked, "Who are you talking to?"

She replied, "Are you going to plow your fields? I'm talking to my husband."

The man looked around and said, "I'm going to plow a barren field. Where is your husband?"

Fourth Wife You replied, "You're going to plow a barren field? My husband died twenty years ago."

The man stared in surprise and said, "Are you sick or delirious? This is crazy talk."

Fourth Wife You replied, "I've never been sick my entire life. My mind has never been clearer than it is now, and I've never been happier."

The man walked away in confusion, but even as he was leaving he kept turning around to look back at her.

By the time Fourth Wife You reached You Village, it was already dusk and the village was bathed in red light. Even the pig troughs and the horse stables outside each house appeared red. Everyone eating their dinner came out to the street holding their rice bowls, gossiping about this and that. An old midwife rushed into the village, whereupon all the villagers realized that they were about to have a new addition. One villager standing at the entrance to the village was holding his rice bowl but he wasn't eating; instead he was staring at the home of the family that was about to give birth. He asked if the baby was going to be a girl or a boy, and noted that you can predict someone's fortune based on where they are born. Children born in the county seat may go on to become government officials, while those born in the provincial seat may go on to study at the university. There was also a granddaughter who, before she had even turned ten, went to the district to represent the township in some competition. As he was saying this, he saw the family's octogenarian grandmother hobble out of an alley, followed by a goat and a dog, and after exchanging a few auspicious remarks with the villagers she proceeded toward the village entrance.

The sunset was warm and tranquil, and the fields were bathed in red light. The grandmother stood motionless in the entrance to the village, gazing out at the road leading into the mountain ridge. The dog and the goat were lying at her feet, as though they were her own grandchildren. At this point, Fourth Wife You came down from the mountain ridge, her face hard, her head and body covered in a layer of dust as thick as a padded jacket. She proceeded quickly, as though she were going somewhere to pick up money or take care of some important business—as though if she were late all would be lost, but if she were on time she could make a fortune. When

Fourth Wife You reached the entrance to the village, the elderly woman stopped her, took two red eggs out of her pocket, and handed them to Fourth Wife You. With an embarrassed smile on her deeply wrinkled face, the woman said, "Fourth Idiot's mother, I've been waiting for you. My grandson's wife is about to give birth."

Fourth Wife You looked at the red eggs, and said, "Congratulations, Fourth Idiot's grandmother! Soon you'll be able to live in a four-generation family."

The old woman said, "I'm glad I've caught you; I think the baby will be a boy. If you agree not to pass in front of our house, my son says he will give you two hundred *jin* of wheat to help you and Fourth Idiot make it through the winter."

Fourth Wife You paused for a moment, her face pale as snow. As she shuddered, the dirt and dust from the journey fell to the ground. She asked coldly, "Why would I not go by your house?"

The old woman said, "I apologize, but what if you pass him some sickness as you go by? If you agree to circle around the other end of the village, then I'll also give you a basket of corn in addition to the wheat."

Fourth Wife You didn't say anything else, and instead she simply stared at the old woman. Fourth Wife You's gaze was hard and her face was dark purple. It seemed as though she could devour the old woman with her gaze or drive her away with her face. But the old woman was, after all, merely an old woman, and she said, "Fourth Wife You, if you agree not to pass in front of our house, I'd be happy to have my children give you some extra money." At this point, all eyes in the street had turned their way, and several were coming over to watch the excitement. Along the mountain ridge, the setting sun sounded like water running over dry desert sand, and in the peace of the village there were explosive sounds of wood burning. The dog and goat stood behind the old woman, gazing expectantly at Fourth Wife You, who slowly shifted her gaze away from the old woman and toward the blood-red street. Without saying a word, she walked past the old woman and down the street, taking large strides that seemed out of proportion with her slight body, as she headed to the entranceway of the old woman's home.

The old woman looked deathly pale, and said, "Fourth Idiot's mother, besides the grain, how about if I give you some more money?"

Fourth Wife You took several more steps, then turned around and threw the red eggs to the dog and the goat.

The old woman said, "Fourth Son's mother, shall I call you Sister, Mother, or Grandmother?" Fourth Wife You didn't look back, and instead looked straight ahead as she walked faster.

Several men approached and stood in the middle of the road, blocking her way.

Fourth Wife You said, "If you don't let me pass this evening, I'll hang myself at your doorstep."

The men slowly stepped aside to let her pass.

With her head up, Fourth Wife You passed through the crowd of men as if pushing through a half-open door. The village street was uncommonly quiet. The chickens, ducks, pigs, and cattle had all returned to their pens, leaving only a handful of villagers still eating in the streets, in the canteen, or in their own doorways. Fourth Wife You's footsteps were loud and heavy. They echoed as she walked down the street, and the afterglow trembled in that sound like a silk sheet. The elderly woman stood blankly behind her, watching as she receded into the distance. Eventually, she approached that old woman's tile-roofed house, and by this point the screams of the woman about to give birth reverberated through the village, like a whirlwind of sand and rocks. The old woman was startled, and she rushed after Fourth Wife You, shouting, "Fourth Idiot's mother, Fourth Idiot's mother!" Just before Fourth Wife You reached the doorway to the old woman's house, the old woman grabbed her and said, "I'm eighty years old, and in another six months I'll be eighty-one. But I'm still willing to kneel down and beg you not to pass by my house." Fourth Wife You turned around and saw that the old woman, her eyes full of tears, was indeed in the process of kneeling down in front of her.

Fourth Wife You's heart softened and she grabbed the old woman, as though grabbing a pole that was about to topple over. She held the woman in front of her, looked at her coldly, and suddenly spat in her face. Then she spun around and walked away. The entire village was silent, and even the dog and the goat stared at Fourth Wife You in surprise. Fourth Wife You's spittle flew like bullets in all directions, splattering the villagers nearby. The old woman stood there in confusion, with phlegm dripping down her face. The other villagers also stood there blankly, and by the time it occurred to them to wipe their faces and curse Fourth Wife You, she had already turned a corner and disappeared from view.

The rivers dried up and the earth had been overturned in the blink of an eye. Fourth Wife You walked stiffly, like a statue carved out of stone. In the alley, a couple of chickens and ducks saw her corning and squawked as they hid by the side of the road, leaving her ample room to pass. She stood for a while at the door to her house, looking toward the center of the village. She heard the new wife's screams as they rippled her way like water, and proceeded to spit a gob of snow-white spittle in their direction—after which she followed the screams into the courtyard.

The front gate, which had been locked, swung open. It turned out that her husband, Stone You, was home waiting for her. Fourth Wife You stepped through the front gate and found Stone You sitting on the doorstep watching Fourth Idiot, as though watching a calf trying to break free of its rope. In the courtyard, there was also a snow-white lamb, and under the tree Fourth Idiot was staring intently at the animal, unable to see that his father was at his side. Fourth Idiot wanted to hug the lamb, kiss it, and caress its head, body, and belly. He also wanted to stroke the animal's tiny red bean-like teats, and touch it where it shouldn't be touched. In the end, however, Fourth Idiot decided the lamb must be very clever, because it would always wait until he was almost in front of it before slipping away. As a result, even though Fourth Idiot chased it like crazy through the courtyard, he could never catch the lamb. What he didn't realize was that Stone You was right next to him, and each time Fourth Idiot was about to catch the lamb, Stone You would go up to the animal and scare it, causing it to run away. Fourth Idiot chased the lamb all afternoon, and by evening he was exhausted. He sat in the middle of the courtyard trying to catch his breath, and Stone You watched over him as Fourth

Idiot stared at the lamb. It was at this point that Fourth Wife You arrived. She stood in the doorway, and Fourth Idiot turned pale.

He said, "Ma, I can't catch the lamb. I want to sleep with it."

Fourth Wife You stood in the entranceway. Her eyes had a greenish tint, and, like a block of ice in winter, she immediately chilled all the warmth from the courtyard's evening sunlight.

Stone You asked, "What's wrong?"

Fourth Wife You bit her purple lips, but didn't respond.

Stone You said, "I originally wanted to go with you to visit Eldest and Second Daughters, but after lunch Fourth Idiot kept chasing someone's heifer all around the village. The villagers began cursing and beating him, and the other village kids picked up rocks and clumps of earth and threw them at his head."

Fourth Wife You shifted her icy stare toward Stone You.

The screams of the woman giving birth once again wafted over, and in the quiet dusk they resembled an early autumn wind scattering red and yellow leaves everywhere.

As Fourth Wife You looked in the direction of those screams and then back at Fourth Idiot, her face gradually acquired a trace of warmth.

She said, "Fourth Idiot, come here."

Like a famished infant who sees a stranger, Fourth Idiot cautiously approached and hid in the embrace of Fourth Wife You, who smoothed down his hair and saw that his head was in fact so swollen and lacerated that it resembled tree bark. Several of his wounds had scabbed over, though the blood continued to flow out from beneath. Fourth Wife You asked, "Why were you chasing the village cattle? Didn't I tell you to stay home and not leave no matter what?"

Fourth Idiot said, "I want to sleep with that cow."

Stone You said, "He was also chasing the chickens and ducks in the village."

Fourth Wife You asked, "Did the chickens and ducks ever bother you?"

Fourth Idiot said, "I want to sleep with the chickens and ducks, and have a baby with them."

As he was saying this, wave after wave of the new bride's cries swept toward them, pushing the setting sun's last rays back over the mountain. In the end, a final bloody scream rent the sky, and the sun disappeared in silence. The village immediately fell quiet, and there wasn't the lightest breath of sound. It was as if the woman about to give birth had fallen asleep, or had passed out from the pain. The entire world had fallen quiet.

Fourth Wife You asked, "Fourth Idiot, why do you want to have a baby?"

Fourth Idiot said, "I want to have a baby so that it can cry for milk."

Fourth Wife You said, "If Mother really does find you a wife, will you be able to give her a baby?"

Fourth Idiot said, "If Ma finds me a wife to hold while I sleep, I'll give Ma a baby, and also make her a black coffin."

Stone You turned pale.

Fourth Wife You said, "Do you want me to find you a wholer wife?"

Fourth Idiot said, "I'll make Ma a coffin out of cypress wood."

Stone You stared at Fourth Idiot and stamped his foot.

Fourth Wife You said, "A wholer wife, and a pretty one, too?"

Fourth Idiot said, "I'll make the coffin from cypress wood, one inch thick."

Stone You turned completely white and kept stamping his foot in front of Fourth Idiot.

Fourth Wife You continued asking questions, and each time she heard Fourth Idiot's answers, her face would lighten. Eventually, she looked as peaceful as a bowl of water tucked beneath a wall so that it is never touched by the wind. In the entranceway a woman walked forward quickly. She said, "Third Auntie, can you guess what she gave birth to? It's a boy! Quick, bring your family's scale. People say that if you hang your scale outside your door for three days, then when the boy grows up and finds a wife, he will end up with the beautiful daughter of the county mayor." Fourth Wife You agreed, and the other woman departed, leaving the You Family courtyard as quiet as the rest of the village. In the mountains, this period just before sunset was the quietest moment of the day, like a cloud fading in the distance. Stone You stamped his feet in front of Fourth Wife You and screamed, "You must beat Fourth Idiot. Slap him! If you don't, he'll only get stupider, and will keep flying in the face of Heaven and Earth." But Fourth Wife You ignored him. Instead, she pushed Fourth Idiot away from her and stared at him for a long time. She saw that he had a clown-like smile on his face, as though Fourth Wife You really was about to find him a wife—as though his new wife was about to appear before him.

The woman who wanted to borrow a scale returned. The banging of the scale's chain and weight sounded like music as she came nearer.

Fourth Wife You said, "Fourth Idiot, repeat to Mother what you just said."

Fourth Idiot said, "If Ma finds me a pretty wife, I'll give her a baby boy, and also make her a coffin from cypress wood."

Fourth Wife You said, "The coffin should be made without any cracks, so that my bones won't decay for decades." She added, "There is something else—tomorrow Mother will prepare some packages, and you should take them to the families of your eldest and third sisters."

Fourth Idiot said, "What am I taking them? The road to their homes is as long as the sky is high."

Fourth Wife You said, "If you deliver the packages, I'll make you a fried bun."

Fourth Idiot said, "I want five fried buns."

Fourth Wife You said, "Then I'll fry five of them."

Fourth Idiot said, "Use extra oil, and also some scallion blossoms."

Fourth Wife You said, "I'll use all of the oil we have left in the barrel."

Fourth Idiot said, "After I finish eating I'll go to sleep and won't go anywhere."

Fourth Wife You paused in surprise and stared at Fourth Idiot's face as though it were a wooden board. A predusk glimmer of sunlight shone down, and Fourth Wife You hurried into the kitchen, grabbed a cleaver, and reemerged. She held it up in front of Fourth Idiot and said with severity, "What am I making you the buns for?"

Fourth Idiot turned pale, and his pupils shrunk until his eyes appeared almost entirely white. He stepped back several paces, saliva dribbling from his trembling lips. He said, "Ma, don't chop me. Let me make you a cypress-wood coffin without any cracks. Then I'll take the two packages to my sisters' families."

Fourth Wife You threw the cleaver down next to a whetstone in the kitchen doorway, and said, "Fourth Idiot, don't be afraid. Mother is going to fry you some buns."

The white receded from Fourth Idiot's eyes and he licked the saliva from his face while watching his mother.

Fourth Wife You headed into the house. After a while, she walked into the kitchen carrying a grain jar with a broken mouth and a barrel full of used oil. She began kneading the dough, and proceeded to dump all of the grain onto the table, whereupon she broke open the bottom of the jar by smashing it against the table. After removing all of the remaining grain, she threw the broken jar to the ground. The sky was almost black by this point, and the village was once again filled with the sound of people walking back and forth. These were men who, after eating, would congregate in the entrance of the village to chat. The women were still at home washing up after dinner, and the bright clinking of dishes circulated through the night. Fourth Wife You lit a lamp, and as she was kneading the dough, her face became covered in white flour. At this point, Stone You walked in, stood in front of her, and said, "If you eat all of the grain you borrowed, what are you going to have tomorrow?" She didn't see him, nor did she answer. The dough in the bowl was a little stiff, so she got two handfuls of water from the water basin. Stone You said, "Something seems to be on your mind. What happened today?" She placed the dough on the table and spread it out, then dumped out the oil in the barrel. She rubbed the inside of the barrel with some dough to remove all of the remaining oil. When the inside of the barrel was finally so clean you could see your reflection in it, she threw the barrel to the ground next to the broken grain jar. She added a pinch of salt to the dough, then another. She hesitated a moment, then added an entire fistful of salt. Stone You cried out, "You're making it too salty! Do you want Fourth Idiot to die of thirst after he eats it?" Fourth Wife You still didn't answer, and instead glanced at Stone You and proceeded to dump all of the remaining salt onto the dough. She was about to throw the salt bucket under the table as well, but hesitated. She turned it upside down and looked at it, saw that there were two cracks in it, then tossed it aside.

Stone You said, "Do you want to die? I don't think you want to live. But if you die, how is Fourth Idiot going to survive?"

Fourth Wife You took some scallions from under the table and peeled them. Without even washing them, she chopped them up and sprinkled them over the dough. Then she squeezed the dough into a spiral and cut it into five portions. As she was doing so, some grains of salt rolled off like peas, and she scooped them up and placed them back on the dough. When she finished, she slowly lifted her head and looked up at Stone You as though seeing someone she didn't recognize. At this point she appeared very calm and full of kindness. A warm glow radiated from her face. The night was as endless as the sky, and a mysterious sound from the fields crept inexorably into the You family courtyard. When Fourth Wife You heard this sound, she dropped her gaze from Stone You's face, so thin and indistinct as to almost not be there, and looked at the one leg Stone You had left, after the other had been taken for Second Daughter. She told Stone You quietly, "Second Daughter has been cured."

He stared in shock.

She said, "Now we cure Eldest Daughter, Third Daughter, and Fourth Idiot."

He stepped back half a step, staring at her in surprise.

She said, "You don't have that many bones left, so let me have a turn." She added, "Tonight you can bring home the butcher from the village next door. I hear he died only yesterday and now is lying on a pallet in the main room of his house. You should bring him over while his body is still warm and his hands still retain some of the strength of a living person. He will know everything." She added, "Sharpen the knife. Fourth Idiot's illness is the worst, so boil my head while it is still warm and then feed it to him. Eldest and Third Daughters' illnesses are not as severe, so you can divide the rest of my bones in two, and then wrap them in three layers of white cloth and place them on the table. After Fourth Idiot becomes a bit more clearheaded, he can take them to his sisters."

The moon came out.

The mountain ridge and the village were both floating in the water-like moonlight. In the You family's courtyard, there was a slight chill, as a yellowish-green autumn breeze blew through, sweeping the chicken feathers and weeds into a pile at the base of the wall. The nocturnal sounds from the fields along the mountain ridge resonated past the kitchen counter, through the stove, and onto the kitchen table. Fourth Wife You had already lit a fire and was furiously pumping the bellows, making a rhythmic sound like a wooden clapper. Stone You left, but before he did he looked at Fourth Wife You and said, "Mother of our four children, you should reconsider. Can't you just use my remaining bones?"

She threw him a look that was half hot and half cold, and asked, "How could that be enough? You've been dead for more than twenty years, and your bones have been decomposing this entire time. Do you even know how much medicine they can yield?"

He said, "You should reconsider. You really should. This is truly a matter of life and death."

She said, "Go fetch that butcher and have him come over tonight. Give him some money, so that you're not asking him to come here for nothing."

He replied, "Mother of our four children, you really must reconsider."

She roared, "Are you going or not? If your ancestors hadn't passed down this disease to us, I wouldn't have to be doing this now."

He didn't answer, and instead quietly backed out of the kitchen and left. Fourth Wife You heated the skillet and placed the greased bun on top, immediately filling the kitchen with the fragrant scent of oil and baked scallions.

In the courtyard, Fourth Idiot shouted, "Ma, are the buns ready? I'm hungry . . ."

Fourth Wife You shouted back, "Fourth Babe, wait just a moment."

She turned down the stove until it was just a single flame, allowing the buns to bake slowly. At this point, Fourth Idiot walked in and looked at the skillet with the buns. He appeared parched, as layers of excitement peeled off his face and fell to the ground, and his shirt was drenched in saliva. Fourth Wife You asked him, "Do you remember everything Mother told you?"

He replied, "Yes, I do."

Fourth Wife You asked, "Will you forget?"

Fourth Idiot replied, "If I forget, Ma can take a cleaver and chop me up."

By this point, the fried buns were ready, and their fragrance filled the kitchen. As Fourth Wife You was removing them from the skillet, Fourth Idiot began gurgling with anticipation, his Adam's apple bobbing up and down. He tried to grab one of the buns, but Fourth Wife You gently pushed his hand away. She cut the bun into quarters, placed them in a bowl, then handed it to him.

Fourth Idiot devoured several bites, and said, "Delicious. Ma, I'll have four and a half of these five buns, and will leave the remaining half for you."

Fourth Wife You placed another bun on the hot skillet, and watched as Fourth Idiot ate ravenously.

After taking several more bites, Fourth Idiot suddenly stopped and said, "Ma, it's salty. It's incredibly salty."

Fourth Wife You relit the stove, and said, "Keep eating. They're good when they're salty."

Fourth Idiot started eating again.

Fourth Idiot ate four and a half buns, one after another. As his belly was filling up, he wanted to drink some water, but Fourth Wife You said that he shouldn't—if he did, his stomach would hurt. Instead, after he finished eating the buns, he should go sleep for a while. Fourth Idiot took several bites from that final bun and handed the remainder to Fourth Wife You, saying, "Ma, would you like some?" Fourth Wife You looked at the row of tooth marks on the bun, like a row of crescent moons. She said, "Fourth Babe, Mother doesn't want any. Why don't you keep it for later?" Fourth Idiot laughed, and placed the bun into his breast pocket. Then he went into the courtyard to look at the closed gate and the full moon, and listen to the sound of villagers heading home to rest. Finally, patting his belly as though it were a drum, he retreated to his room.

Fourth Idiot entered his room, climbed into bed, and went to sleep.

The village's peacefulness was tall and thick, except for the silver-chain cries of the crickets, which echoed through the streets and alleys. The fields outside the village were also full of the cries of nocturnal creatures, which sounded like the rustling of silk. The stars were somewhat sparse, though the moon was so full it looked as though it might burst. In the moonlight, you could occasionally see some ants and other insects out for a midnight stroll. Fourth Idiot had been watching intently, but as soon as he went to bed he immediately fell into a deep sleep.

Even then, his hands resting on his swollen belly, he continued to grip that final half of a fried bun.

Fourth Wife You emerged from the kitchen and leaned up to Fourth Idiot's window to peer in. She picked up a shovel that had fallen down and set it against the wall, then hung the hoe from a wooden beam. She took the sickle that was on the window ledge and stuck it into a crack in the wall, then returned to the kitchen, where she carefully overturned the cistern and poured out all the water inside. Then she poured out the water bucket into the courtyard, too. Finally, she poured out all of the remaining water in the house, so that not a drop was left, and only then did she leave.

By this point, the rest of the village was sound asleep, and from the streets you could hear the faint sounds of people snoring in their rooms. In the cattle pens there was the coarse sound of cattle breathing, while the warm smell of fresh grass wafted through the village streets and alleys. The village dogs were also sleeping deeply, undisturbed by the occasional sounds coming from the village or the mountain ridge. Fourth Wife You stood in her doorway gazing up at the sky. Then she anxiously walked toward the village entrance, arriving at the large gate tower that she hadn't passed through the preceding evening. Its doors tightly shut, the structure stood proud under the moonlight. The two large "Happiness" characters that had been posted there during the previous year's New Year's festival were still clearly visible in the night light.

Fourth Wife You stood in front of the gate tower, staring at it in a daze.

After a moment, she began loudly singing just as she had done after being married into the You household more than thirty years earlier. She sang:

Tonight the maid lifts her head
Because now she, too, has her own embroidery room
Whereas she was previously a maid, she is now a wife
And now she can order her maid around, just like a young wife
Hey, little Lian, come massage my feet!

Her voice gradually increased in volume, going from dark to bright, and by the time she reached the final line, "Hey, little Lian, come massage my feet," she was roaring. The entire village was awakened by her shouts, which rang through the peaceful and empty mountain ridge like a thunderstorm, and in no time at all had covered the earth in water. Several dogs came running out and stood in the middle of the street, barking madly. Some people opened their front doors and stuck their heads out. Amidst all of the ruckus, someone's rooster began crowing, and the cattle asleep in their pens also stood up. The entire village awoke with a start, as the newborn baby's cries surged through the cracks in the doors, down the streets, and out into the fields.

Fourth Wife You sang her song twice in front of the gate tower, and continued as she walked toward the village entrance.

In the entrance, she saw Stone You and someone else whose face she couldn't make out walking down from the mountain ridge. At that point, she abruptly stopped singing and returned home, and only after she returned home did she finish the song. Then, she stretched up to the window to check on Fourth Idiot. When she saw he was sleeping soundly, she proceeded to the central room and slowly folded the sheets, blankets, and bedding, placing them in a neat bundle for Fourth Idiot to use when he got married. She looked around the room, hung an oil lamp from the wall, then moved the sewing kit from the table to the lid of the box. Next, she wiped the dust from the bed and slowly lay down. As she lay down she seemed to slide on the bed, and a noisy chill seeped into her spine. It was then that she remembered the mat on the bed was a new one that had been placed there at the beginning of the year. She got up and rolled up the mat, put it next to the wall, then looked around the room before slowly lying down again on the hard wooden bed frame. She slammed her eyelids shut like a pair of city gates.

Time rumbled forward like a flour mill.

The sound of footsteps drifted into her room like a specter.

Eventually, a shout in the front room was violently suppressed—like a leaf that had just been picked up by the wind, only to run into the wall or a closed door. The courtyard, village, and the entire mountain ridge suddenly became as peaceful as a lake after a boat has sunk beneath the surface. The entire world seemed to go back into a dream.

Fourth Idiot was awakened in the middle of the night by an acute thirst. He dreamed he was entering a furnace, as his stomach was dried up and his throat was on fire. After gulping for air several times, he woke up, jumped out of bed, and rubbed his eyes. When he went to the kitchen to get some water, he discovered that there wasn't a single drop left in the cistern. When he went to the bucket, he found that it was lying upside down on the ground. He then went to the washbasin, which usually had half a bowl of water, but all he saw was the reflection of the moon in the bottom of the basin. He couldn't find a single drop of water in the entire kitchen. He kicked the cistern and the bucket, then grabbed the washbasin and threw it to the ground as well. Finally, he went into the courtyard and shouted in the direction of the main room.

"Ma . . . you're making me die of thirst . . . Ma, you're deliberately making me die of thirst."

Hearing no response, he pushed open the door to the main room, walked in, and saw his mother lying peacefully in bed. On the bedside table there was a bowl of dark red soup. Without saying a word, Fourth Idiot stepped forward, grabbed the bowl, and drank its contents. There was a thick, dark red taste in his mouth, throat, stomach, and intestines, which spread between his sinews and his bones. On the verge of vomiting, he noticed that on the table there were two bowl-like white bags. As he was reaching out to open one, he saw lying on it the cleaver with which his mother had frightened him the night before. He suddenly remembered that his mother had asked him to take the contents of the two bags to his eldest and third sisters.

And so, before dawn, he carried the two bags into the depths of the Balou Mountains.

Chapter Seven

They didn't bury Fourth Wife You until half a month later.

Her pallbearers were her son and three sons-in-law, while her eldest, second, and third daughters followed behind, wailing. When the other villagers came to help with the funeral, they discovered that Fourth Idiot's illness was completely cured, and he was now as clearheaded as everyone else. Moreover, the three daughters standing beside their mother's corpse were all pregnant. They had all become wholers and were now beautiful and neatly dressed, even as they cried inconsolably. They had each prepared a present for their mother. Eldest Daughter brought three sets of winter burial shrouds made of cotton, Second Daughter brought three sets of summer burial shrouds made of silk, while Third Daughter brought her three sets of spring and autumn clothing she had sewn herself, together with origami figures of virgin children of good fortune, mountains of gold, and silver chariots. Fourth Wife You's four children, who had all become as clearheaded as ordinary people, borrowed money to buy some wooden boards, and then asked someone to make her an inch-and-a-half thick coffin made out of cypress wood. On the day of the burial, Stone You and his neighbors in the graveyard went to meet Fourth Wife You, but her four children crowded around the coffin, crying their eyes out. As the coffin was being placed in the grave, it was impossible to tear away Fourth Wife You's children, as one after another they threw themselves onto the lid of the coffin.

Stone You asked, "Do you think you can bring your mother back to life with your crying?"

They all kept crying.

Fourth Wife You said, "This illness is hereditary. Do all of you know how to treat your own children?"

When they heard this, they abruptly stopped crying.

They buried Fourth Wife You's body to the right of Stone You's.